A Daughter's Journey

MYRA LEE GLASS

Coleche Press, Dallas TX

A Daughter's Journey
By Myra Lee Glass

Published by

Coleche Press
Dallas, Texas 75205

Editing by Cynde Christie, WritingCoachCynde.com
Cover and interior layout by Nick Zelinger, NZGraphics.com

ISBN: 979-8-9860315-0-7 (print)
LCCN: data on file

First Edition

Printed in the United States of America

For Father,
Who now has another author in the family.

For Somie,
Who will get to add another book to her
many aesthetic bookshelves.

For Atty,
Who hopefully finds interest in books
through reading this one.

For Jake,
Who found out I was writing this two days ago.

For my Mom,
Who was watching down on me during this
whole journey.

1

Leaning against the side of my house, I stood with my hand to my chest as I caught my breath. I could always stay outdoors for a long time, but it was becoming warmer every day. Our house was old and normally well maintained, but small nicks in the windows and wooden pickets coming loose from the gate were a long time coming. The fiery South Carolina sun had bleached our blue front door and I had to tug on it to get it to open. The spiders on the porch light formed cobwebs and there were no plants in the flowerpots. With Mother pregnant and Father working additional jobs, our home had become a little disorderly.

As I stood my old chipped red bike against a tree, the tires whistled as they slowly ran out of air. I noticed papers peeking out of the mailbox, and grimaced from the squeaky sound while I opened the lid to grab them.

I walked through the front door and noticed that Mother had already begun to try to cook supper. She was an amazing cook, and always had warm treats ready for Father when he arrived home from work.

Unfortunately, her household tasks had become increasingly difficult. Mother was so pregnant; it was a challenge for her even to reach into the high shelf of a cupboard.

A sudden loud crashing noise came from behind her as a stack of metal bowls tumbled down from the table, spinning on the ground with a horrifying scraping noise.

I quickly ducked under the table by mother's feet to pick them up, hitting my head on the side of the table as I stood back up. A single plate fell off the table, shattering into miniscule pieces on the wooden floor.

"Dear God, Estelle, you scared me!" Mother exclaimed, frantically turning around with an empty tray in her hands. "The next time you decide to walk in unannounced, expect those bowls to hit you in the head."

I giggled, placing the bowls back onto the table. "Mother, like you would let them hit me."

She smiled, "If you frighten me again like that, I might as well!" She turned back around to face the counter, setting down the tray. I watched her as she grabbed the pitcher of tea; her hands trembled as she tried to pour it into a glass. She grimaced.

"Here, let me help you with that." I offered, rushing over to her. She jerked her hands away as I tried to grab the heavy pitcher away from her. The tea spilled over the pitcher and down her stomach, wetting her apron and dress.

"Shoot," Mother whispered under her breath, "I- I just don't know what's been happening recently."

I rushed to grab a towel, and placed it on her wet stomach. "You just need to take it easy, Mother." She looked almost defeated, very unlike herself.

"Estelle–"

"Mother," I interrupted. Even though it seemed that even a single gust of wind could knock her over, I saw a hint of determination on her face. "Let me help you with the rest of dinner, Father should be back any minute."

She placed her hand over my own on her stomach, pressing down on the towel. "I am not going to rely on you like this when I have the baby, Estelle."

"I know, I know, Mother. But you need to right now." I poured the rest of the tea into three glasses, and placed them on the dining table. As I set the rest of the table, I glanced over and saw her staring blankly out of the window. "Why don't you just sit down at the table, I can make the plates for you while you rest." I told her.

She shook her head, looking away from the window. She leaned over the counter on her hands, staring down into the sink solemnly. "Do you remember when you were so small; you could fit into the cupboard under the sink?" She asked, refusing to look at me.

I took in a breath, not knowing how to respond. "I remember it being very dark, but I don't remember much."

She lifted her head, sighing heavily while wiping her eyes. "During loud thunderstorms, you would run through the house screaming." She walked over to the table, pulling out a chair and sitting down heavily. "Whenever you heard the thunder crash, you would squeeze yourself down into the cupboard and have your father and I close the doors for you." She looked up at me. "It was the only way to get you to stop crying. It was dark enough that you couldn't see the lightning, and it made you feel secure."

Her tears streamed down her face as she nervously played with her hands. "After the storms would clear up, your father and I would take you outside and look up at the sky with you. We would show you that the storms and clouds were gone, and point out all of the stars. We would sit out there for hours just staring, taking in the moment. There were times where you were so still that I thought you were asleep, but when I would look over at you to check on you, I would see you just staring up at the stars."

My eyes started welling up with tears as I sat in the chair next to her. She grabbed my hands and placed them into her lap.

"I love you, Mother," I told her. "And I already love the new baby."

"I love you, too." She whispered, taking my hands and pulling them towards her. She placed them on her stomach and closed her eyes. I shut mine as well, and we sat there in silence as I felt the baby kick.

"Oh, wow!" I smiled, looking up at her.

"Can you feel him kicking?" She asked, smiling through her tears. "He's been doing this a lot recently."

"He?"

"I hope so," she laughed, looking down at the ground. "I already have the most wonderful daughter I could ask for."

I smiled and felt the tears coming back to my eyes. I loved her so much.

I heard the front door open with a creak, and a deep voice call out. "Mary?" The voice made its way toward the kitchen. Mother quickly wiped her tears and stood up, wobbling as she used the edge of the table to stand. Father stood by the entryway, looking exhausted.

"Hello, John." She smiled.

"How are you feeling?" He looked at mother. She slowly treaded towards him, reaching for his arm.

She panted. "Just a little tired." He placed his hand on her shoulder and cupped his other hand on her cheek. It seemed that Father was almost holding her up, and they looked at each other for a few moments. Mother gave him a quick kiss and they continued to hold each other for a while. I groaned, raising my eyebrows as I looked away.

Mother turned her head to face me as Father closed his eyes. "Estelle!" She hollered, "Don't be impolite. You'll love someone someday as well."

I pursed my lips and widened my eyes. "Not for a long, long time." I told them. Mother sighed and Father helped her to the table. I began to stare at the ground, my fingers fidgeting.

"Will you bring supper to the table?" Mother asked as Father pulled out her chair. She sat down with a thud and scooted her chair close to the edge. "Estelle," Mother snapped her fingers to gain my attention. "Quickly, we don't want it to get cold."

I stood up and wandered over to the stove, dramatically pushing my chair in. Father shook his head at me. I grabbed the pan of green beans off our gas stove, pouring them onto a plate. A basket of blueberries lay in the sink, and I rinsed them off to put into a bowl. I set them in the center of the dining table, over the light blue tablecloth. Our kitchen was basic but pretty, with a circle table in the center and three dark wooden chairs around it. The fourth chair lived in the closet next to Mother and Father's room because the screws had become loose. Father had been a bit distracted with his additional jobs, and Mother always nagged him to hire some-one to fix it. The floor was checkered white and blue tile, scratched and old. The window above the sink looked out over the yard, and had white curtains draped on either side of it. Mother liked to collect little clay birds when we travel, and they sat atop the windowsill.

"Honey, would you grab some extra knives?" Mother called, "The chicken might be a little tough." I nodded, reach-ing over to counter. It had little drawers on the side where we kept silverware and the nice utensils we used for Christmas dinner. The drawer opened with a pop, the silverware clanging loudly inside of it.

Father looked over at me. "Easy on the furniture," he muttered. "We don't want those drawers any more broken because it will be a little while until I have the time to fix them."

I closed my eyes in frustration. "I got it." I mumbled so he wouldn't hear. Father rarely had any free time because he had taken on extra jobs to save money for the baby. I grabbed three knives and set them by the plates.

"So how was your day, Honey?" Father asked mother quietly, glancing between her and I.

"Fine."

"Good."

Mother and I peeked at each other, not knowing which one of us was supposed to answer. Father chuckled, "Well, I hope the both of you had a good day." He reached for a stack of paper and envelopes that I placed on the edge of the table. "Is this today's mail?"

Mother nodded. "Estelle just got it." She took a sip of her tea and as she swallowed said, "Looks like more than we usually receive."

I slipped Mother's red oven mitts onto my hands and pulled out a hot tray with three pieces of chicken. I saw father reach for the newspaper and unfold it. I placed the tray onto the stove and started plating the chicken while Father read from the paper.

"Saturday, June 4, 1938." He mumbled, reading the rest under his breath. I walked over to the table balancing three plates on my hands, placing each one on the table. Mother flipped through the rest of the mail, picking one out of the pile and setting it aside. I pulled my chair back out and sat down while Father tilted his glasses up to get a better look at the paper.

"So," I began, digging my fork into the chicken. "ViVi and I were thinking that we could have a picnic by Beaufort River tomorrow morning." Mother glanced at Father.

"ViVi?" Father looked up from the paper.

"Vivian" I responded, "from school." I saw Mother eye him.

"Mr. Massey's daughter?" He asked. The Masseys always sat behind us in church. He turned to Mother. "What do you think, Mary?"

Mother sat down the pile of mail and placed her napkin in her lap. "Well," She paused, peering back up at Father. "I think that's a lovely idea."

Father smiled at me.

"If you go down early, you might find some pretty birds." She suggested.

"Thank you!" I exclaimed as I picked up a handful of blueberries and set them on my plate. Mother continued to eat as Father folded up the newspaper. He leaned over his plate when he noticed the letter that Mother had set aside.

"Who sent this letter, Mary?" Father asked as he reached for the envelope. Mother set her fork down before she plucked the letter from his fingers and held it to her chest.

"My sister." She said in a slow tone, watching Father's expression closely. They continued to maintain eye contact until Mother broke it, setting the letter on the table beside her napkin. I could hear Father inhale, and then watched as he closed his eyes and sighed.

He focused back on Mother and smiled slightly. "What did she write you about? Has anything happened in Boston?"

"I'm not sure yet. But I am glad that she is finally deciding to write to us." She ripped the top edge of the envelope. As she began to read, I glanced between the two of them and examined my Father's expression. I knew that he and Aunt Rose weren't fond of each other. "Dear Mary and Family," Mother read aloud. Father smirked, reaching for his newspaper to read once more. Mother took a pause to examine Father's expression, and then went back to reading the letter without any other distractions. She read the rest of the letter silently, periodically glancing up at Father.

"What else did she say?" I urged. Although I didn't know Aunt Rose very well, I knew she was wealthy and lived up in Boston, Massachusetts.

"Oh, well nothing, really." She gave me a sweet smile. "She just wants to check up on us and the baby."

"Us or just the baby?" Father said between his teeth, flipping through the newspaper.

Mother dropped her knife; the silverware clanging made me jump in my seat. "Us, all of us." Mother answered in a stern tone. I scanned between the two of them, and I noticed that both of their moods had suddenly changed. "She asked how her niece was doing, John. You know she doesn't have any family except for us."

"That would be because that heinous woman couldn't start a family of her own." Father stated while staring intensely at one spot of his newspaper. My eyes widened while Mother pursed her lips. I sat holding my fork midair, waiting for what they would say next.

"John," Mother said in a hushed tone. "Not right now." Mother began to stand up, grunting as she gripped onto my shoulder tightly. Mother took in a heavy breath, squeezing her eyes closed.

Father's eyes quickly turned to Mother. "Mary!" He stood from the table, his body pushing his chair backwards forcefully towards the kitchen wall. He rushed towards her, his hands grabbing her shoulder to hold her up. Mother held onto his arms, one of her hands gripping his arm and the other wrapped tight around her lower abdomen.

I dropped my fork and launched myself out of my chair, bolting towards them in a panic. "Mother! Mother!" I looked at Father for help, my mind racing.

"John…" Mother gasped, trying to spit her words out. "John, the baby!" She closed her eyes, her face full of pain from the contractions. Father's muscles tightened, and in a low voice demanded, "Estelle, grab the hospital pack." I nodded at him with a confused look, searching around the kitchen with my eyes for the pack. He tightened his grip on Mother, lifting his chin in the direction of the hallway. My eyes widened as I sprinted through the kitchen doorway, leading out into the hall. I pushed Mother and Father's bedroom door open with a bang. The room, lit with a dim light, made it hard to see anything. I quickly ruffled through the dresser, a million thoughts shooting through my mind. *Will Mother be okay? Why has this happened so suddenly?*

Where is the hospital pack? A small blue bag was next to Mother's night table; I could see a nightgown and socks inside of it. I swiftly grabbed it, my heart beating out of my chest with adrenaline. I could hear Mother's groans from the kitchen, causing tears to swell in my eyes. I raced out of the room and went back into the hallway, watching Father as he opened the front door.

"Let me put the pack in the car and we can hurry to the hospital!" I cried out, running past Mother and Father onto the porch.

"Estelle!" Father yelled behind me. I turned to face him and Mother, my chest rising up and down. "We need you to stay here." He told me with a steady voice.

My stomach dropped. The tears that I held trapped in my eyes finally started to slowly flow down my cheeks as my jaw tightened and my brows furrowed in disbelief.

"I don't understand." I told them, running back up the porch steps to face them.

Father placed a hand on my cheek, running his thumb back and forth. He tilted his head and looked solemnly into my eyes. "Honey, we will be back tomorrow afternoon." He brushed his fingers through my hair, my tears falling onto his hand.

"John. We need to go, right now." Mother looked up at him. Her head rested on his shoulder. Her eyes found me, and her arm reached out to caress my neck. "I love you, Estelle." She took a deep breath in. "I will see you soon, sweetie."

Father squeezed my shoulder as he and Mother stumbled past me, down the porch steps. I stood with my shoulders dropped and my knees weak, facing the doorway they had just stepped out. I saw Father as he helped Mother into the passenger seat, her expression full of struggle. He walked around the car, and hopped quickly into the driver's seat, and closed the car door and started the engine. The sun had begun to set, and the night sky was getting closer and closer. A cool breeze came over me, and I stood on the front porch step, watching my parents drive off in silence.

2

Jerry cried out as I held him, his newborn body kicking in my arms. He face, flushed and damp with tears, craved Mother. I attempted to adjust him, trying to keep his unsteady head from flinging back and forth. His high-pitched shrieks startled me, and my shushing did not help him quiet down. I stood beside Mother and Father's bed, sneaking glances at Mother. She had been in bed for days, ever since she gave birth to Jerry. She refused to get up for breakfast, so I served it to her while Father and I took turns caring for Jerry. I rocked Jerry back and forth once more, bouncing up and down on the balls of my feet. It was dark in the room even though it wasn't even late afternoon.

Mother had become sensitive to what seemed like everything and everyone, closing the curtains throughout the day to keep the sunlight out. She had almost stopped acknowledging Father and me completely, every so often answering us with only minimal effort. Jerry began to respond to my method of quieting him, his eyes drifting into sleep. I quietly placed him into his bassinet, the one that Mother was once so delighted to get for him. She had spent days picking out the perfect one, only to act as if she didn't even see it when the baby actually arrived. Mother laid on her side under the covers, facing away from me. She had wrapped herself up in so many blankets; I didn't understand how she didn't sweat to death in the middle of June heat and humidity.

I snuck out of the room, hoping to find Father sitting in the living room. He was lying on the couch, his eyes closed, his arms raised about his head twisting his ring with his fingers. He had a weary expression on his face, and mumbled to himself under his breath. Our family living room had a pale green couch against the wall, with a matching chair facing it on the other side of the room. A wooden bookshelf stood near the back door, with our radio placed on its own special shelf. Yellow wallpaper lined the walls, and white curtains draped over the windows. Straight through the windows, you could see the magnolia trees, their white flowers had bloomed in the sun. A blue and red floral rug lay over the wooden floors, dents created in it from the furniture.

I walked over to Father, resting the palm of my hand on the top of his shoulder. He startled awake, catching his breath he howled, "What's happening?" He looked around, his hands searching for his glasses that sat beside his legs on the couch. He swiftly put them on his face, his eyes squinting to get a better view of me and the room. I stood in front of him, my hands glued to my side with my shoulders up to my ears. My lips folded under my teeth as I sucked in my breath.

I exhaled loudly, "Nothing! Everything is okay!" I swallowed hard, eyeing Father as he stood from up the couch. He bounced up and down on his feet, cracking his knuckles before he smoothed down his clothes.

"How is Jerry?" He asked impatiently, clearing his throat. Dark circles loomed under his eyes and his eyelids looked very heavy.

I rubbed my index finger and thumb together. "He is fine, Father. I finally got him down for a nap. I think Mother is napping as well."

"Your Mother's still asleep?" He questioned desperately, leaning towards me, his face full of worry.

"She has been for hours!" I responded. He drew out a quick breath before briskly turning around. He started for the door, continuing to whisper to himself. He reached the hallway, his forearms strained as he stretched out his arm towards his and Mother's bedroom door, I rushed out of the living room and through the hallway, quickly trailing behind him.

"Stop!" I said in a hushed but direct tone. "They're both asleep. I do not want to stay in there all morning again!" His head turned back to look at me, his eyes widening as he took in what I said.

"Estelle. You do not talk to me like that." His jaw moved, tightening as he turned back to the door. Quietly he mumbled, "Especially with everything going on."

I paused at that. I tilted my head I as I uttered, "Everything that's been going on?" I looked down at my feet, my voice shaking, "You mean everything that has been going on with Mother?" I looked back up, my eyes locking into his, questioning.

His fists tightened. "Your Mother is not very happy right now, Estelle." He huffed. He fidgeted with his ring once more, he seemed like he was barely breathing at all. He wasn't telling me what was truly wrong, and that is what I really wanted to know.

"I know that, I can see it for myself!" I pushed myself closer to him, almost into him. Tears welled at my eyes; I felt my cheeks flushing red with desperation. "I am worried, Father!" I yelled with my eyebrows raised so high they started to ache. "I cannot keep caring for Jerry instead of her. Or even you!" I pleaded, grabbing at his wrists. My grip on him was so tight my fingers started to turn white, becoming cold.

"Dear Lord!" He snapped through his teeth. He bent down to become eye level with me. "You need to hush, child!" He strained his neck to get even closer to me; I could almost feel the sweat coming off him. "Your mother cannot hear this." He twisted his wrists out of my grasp, causing me to fall forward. He grunted as if he was simply annoyed with me, he held me up, and pulled me into the hallway.

I heard swift footsteps following behind me. He raised his voice, "Your mother!" I stopped in my tracks, turning my entire body around. He leaned over with one hand on his knee, the other on his hip. He caught his breath, his eyes peering up at me. Finally, he stood back up. He walked towards me as if I was a scared kitten he was trying to rescue. Outstretching his hands to me, he grabbed my forearms. He held onto them gently.

"Your mother," he repeated. "She is experiencing a lot of emotions right now."

I nodded at him, pulling one of my arms away to wipe my tears.

"You have to know that Jerry is our miracle baby. He really is." He smiled bitterly.

"After you were born," he took in a breath. Because of the commotion, the hallway light was still unlit. He looked at the lamp, deciding whether to walk over and turn it on.

"Go on." I told him quietly. I smiled, trying to ease the tension in the room.

His eyes followed my voice back to me, his head still facing in the direction of the lamp. Father's look changed from exasperation to sorrow. "We lost baby, after baby, after baby." He stood still, allowing me to process. *They lost their children? I'm here, aren't I?* My brows furrowed, my body began to shake.

"What do you mean?" I stuttered. I backed away slowly, my arms slipping out of his hands.

"Estelle…" He reached to take my arms back.

"I don't understand what you mean!" I felt like I couldn't get him to listen to my words. I slammed my arms down by my waist. He stood in front of me, speechless.

"Oh, come on Estelle," his voice getting louder. He drew his head farther back from me, his eyes bulging. "Listen to me, please!" His exasperated breath shaking, "Your Mother had pregnancy loses." Father used a stern, serious voice. "She had multiple when you were just a small child."

My expression turned to confusion. "Then why isn't she overjoyed with Jerry? He's here with us, *I'm* here with us!" My lips began to shake again, this time with pure rejection and sadness. "She hasn't spoken to me in weeks! You barely have time for me!" I shook my head as my scowl turned into a long frown. My mouth was stuck open, no words coming out. I couldn't figure this out. I squeezed my eyes shut; hoping Father wouldn't see me cry again.

"Her emotions are different after having a baby, Estelle." He finally began to seem understanding. "Her moods are going to change, for better or for worse."

"When will they get better? I want her to get better." I silently began to cry again, standing still and defeated.

"I don't know– I really don't." Father turned to embrace me. My face pressed against his chest, his hug making me cry harder. I squeezed him with all my might, hoping I would never have to let him go.

Light footsteps came from behind us, causing Father to let go of me.

Mother appeared in the doorway, her eyes tired and bloodshot. She was dressed in a pink nightdress with white lace at the collar and hem.

A beaming smile lit up my face. "Mother!" I wanted so badly to run over and give her a giant hug, but she seemed frail and tired.

She gave us a light smile, her energy non-existent. "Good morning, Honey." Father rushed over to her and gave her a quick kiss on the cheek. She cupped his cheek with her palm, holding it there for a few seconds. As he reached out to her, she pushed his arm down with a soft pat, interlocking her right arm with his left.

The smile stood on my face, taking in the image of Mother finally out of bed. "How are you feeling?" I inched closer to her.

"Good, Honey." I smiled at her again, but she turned away from me. She leaned her head into father's neck, whispering into his ear. He looked up at me, then turned back to her and nodded. Father gave me a curt smile before he walked Mother back into their room.

A few moments of uneasy stillness passed before I heard Father's voice rise, my heart sank in my chest. I crept towards their door, tentatively placing my ear against the center of it.

"She wrote to offer this to me, John." Mother sniffled, her voice tremulous and slow. I jumped as I heard a dresser drawer slam.

"Mary! Your life is here." I heard Father plead. "We have kids! We have a house!"

"Oh, John!" She responded sharply, the quickest I heard her speak in weeks. "I am not abandoning you." A fast zipping noise came from the room.

"Well, it sure feels like you are."

"I am telling you, John, I am not."

"I want you to tell that to Estelle and Jerry!" That was the strongest his voice had gotten. "I want you to tell that to Estelle when she watches you walk down the porch steps."

My hands began to shake as I guided them towards the doorknob. I stood as still as I could in the overwhelming silence.

Mother inhaled, "There is something wrong here, and I will be going to Boston to find out just what that is: to make myself better, to make our family better."

All my weight shifted into the door. It swung open with a blast of air, my feet tripping over themselves. I met Mother's startled gaze while I was kneeling on the ground. My arm still gripped hard onto the doorknob, the full force of my body pushing the door into the wall.

Father's head nodded as he pursed his lips. I couldn't hear him breathing, his body rigid. "You can deal with this, Mary." He inched between the doorframe and me, his arms gravitating towards the back of his neck.

"Mother?" I propelled myself back up, brushing the sides of my dress back down.

Her faced fumed red with panic. "Honey, let me explain!" She was holding tight to a leather duffle bag, clothes spilling out of the top.

"Explain what?" I questioned. "What is going on?" My fingers rubbed the fabric of my dress, right by my hips.

She smiled nervously at me. "Your Aunt Rose has invited me to stay with her in Boston for a little while."

My entire body went numb. "Only you?"

She cautiously walked toward me. "You see Honey, Rose knows a doctor there that can help me."

"Why do you need a doctor to help you with the baby?" My voice teetered.

Her voice became sweet. "The doctor will help me learn how to deal with myself. I won't be gone long, just a few weeks. I will write to you every day. I promise." She clasped the duffle bag shut and headed for the doorway.

"Mother, wait!" I called after her. I turned swiftly in the doorway to look back at her. I chased after her in the hallway. "Mother," I called. "Why can't we go along with you?" Her legs stopped running when she heard me.

She was running out of breath. "Rose wrote that the Doctor advised me to go alone."

I felt light headed, staring at her in disbelief. "I will tell Aunt Rose all about you and Jerry, and everything that has been happening lately."

Footsteps came from the kitchen, quickly disappearing into the bedroom. Father walked out cradling Jerry. "Mary, you don't have to do this. We can find a good doctor for you here; you can stay with your family."

Mother ignored him and headed straight for the front door. She adjusted her yellow dress and jacket that had grown too big to fit her. She carried her over packed duffle bag on her shoulder, limping under the weight of it.

"Stay with your family, Mary!" Father bellowed, his face bright red. Jerry awoke in his arms, shrieking in distress.

Mother opened the door and stepped out onto the porch.

The stars shone brightly, the moon reflecting down onto her. She scurried down the steps, heading for the road.

"Mother!" I yelled out, sprinting to the door and holding myself up with the doorframe. "Mother, come back!"

"Mary! Please!" Father stood behind me. Jerry began to scream, his cries filling up the sky. "Mary, you will not walk to the station!" Father's voice strained.

"I have to, John! I am going!" She yelled from the street. Father and I stepped onto the porch, watching her. Wet tears fell onto my cheeks.

"Mother!" I bawled. My face was hot and I was sweaty. Even with the warm June air, goosebumps grew all over my body.

She continued back down the street, turning her head only to say, "When I come home, everything will be better. This is for the best, I promise." She kept eye contact with me. Moving her gaze to Father she mouthed, "I love you."

Her steps grew quiet as she trudged down the road. I felt Father's presence behind me, soft sniffles coming from him. Jerry continued to scream, his feet kicking and arms flailing in Father's tight grip. Sporadic sobs escaped my throat. Crickets chirped loudly in the trees as if they, too, were calling out to Mother. Small lightening bugs escaped the bushes, their light flickering throughout the front yard. The porch's wooden floorboards creaked as Father turned to head back inside. I stayed in place, studying the road where Mother last stood.

3

I heard birds chirping from the yard as I opened the kitchen window, letting in the warm early morning air. Father's eyes fluttered open, his head resting on the dining table. "Good morning, Father." I walked over to him, patting him on the back. He stirred, lifting his head from the table to look up at me.

"Oh, dear," He rubbed his eyes with his knuckles and fiddled around for his glasses. "Honey, what time is it?"

"Ten o'clock." I replied. The sun had already risen, shining in across the room. Father heaved himself up from his chair, his hand scrambling over the tabletop, now covered with a multitude of old letters. Next to the letters was a notebook with a series of numbers written on it.

"What have you been doing all night?" I questioned. Father had never been a night owl, so finding him to have been awake at all hours of the night was quite a surprise.

"Sorting through the lot of these," he gestured to the pile. I tilted my head at it. "Finding addresses, phone numbers…

anything I can." Father's mood had begun to go bad just like Mother's had, after she left.

"Well, I was wondering if I could spend the day with Vivian, and you could take Jerry." I inched backwards from him. He sighed, spreading his eyebrows with his thumb and finger. "I don't know, Estelle."

"It's just," I began to speak in one breath. "I feel like I've become Jerry's caretaker, and I know that with Mother gone you need the extra help, but I just want one day to go out with Vivian, and I know you are staying in the house today," I could feel my eyes going wide as my words grew quicker. I gulped in a lungful of air and exhaled slowly. "Please?" Father stared down at me, his face frowning.

"I understand, Estelle. I do."

"Oh, thank you!" My chest alleviated. A smile grew across my face.

He raised his shoulders, "But," My smile dropped. "I have been very worried about your mother."

An aching arose in my stomach. "Has she finally respond to our letters, can I read them? Is she okay?" I was aware Mother had been taking ages to write back, but with the distance between Beaufort and Boston I assumed it was normal.

"I haven't heard from her recently, and as I was reading back the letters between her and your aunt I became worried." He said this all very calmly, trying to ease my franticness. "I found Aunt Rose's telephone number and I was going to head out to the post office to call and check in."

"But can't you bring Jerry with you?" I pleaded. "I haven't had a day to myself, and he's getting older!"

"I don't know, Estelle," He was still standing by the table; a few envelopes had drifted in between his fingers. "I planned on leaving him here with you."

I became increasingly annoyed, my foot bouncing on the tile floor. "What if you take Jerry with you, and you're gone so quickly that Vivian and I only have the chance to ride our bikes around the street once." I raised my eyebrows at him, proud of my compromise. "You can trust me Father!" I smiled, "This will be a great time between Father and son at," I giggled, trying to lighten the mood, "the post office!"

Father's face remained serious. "Honey, this is important."

"Don't you just think it's the distance, Father? Mother's with Aunt Rose." Anxiety started to fill my chest again. "She is safe, right? With Aunt Rose?" I backed away, beginning to pant.

Father's voice suddenly trembled. "I don't want to worry you, darling." He stuttered, biting his lip. "But I am not quite sure."

My mind and body froze. He draped his arm around me protectively. "We're going to figure this out Estelle, I promise. I'll call Aunt Rose." I closed my eyes as I buried my face into his chest. Sniffles had begun to escape my nose. We stood there for a few seconds more before we heard a knock at the door. Father jolted at the sound, tightening his grip around me. The knocking grew louder.

"Hello?" A small voice came from the entryway as the front door creaked open. "Estelle, are you home?" The voice turned into light footsteps heading towards the kitchen. "Sorry, I didn't mean to burst in like this," Vivian stopped in the hallway, a small yelp breaking free.

"Oh my goodness Mr. Banks," panicked, she looked between Father and I with wide eyes. "I– I am so sorry– I just came to find Estelle."

"Don't worry," Father muttered towards her. He turned to stand facing me, his back to Vivian who was standing like a frightened cat in the doorway. "Estelle, I think it would be best if you spend some time with your friend here." He became very stern, looking at me to agree with him.

I nodded my head at him, and he nodded back at me. "Are you sure, Father? We need to make sure everything is well with Mother."

He placed his hands on my shoulders like he always does, this time they were there for reassurance. "I'll walk Jerry up to the post office, call Aunt Rose and your mother. Go ahead and go out with your friend, but be quick."

"I will, I promise."

Father shuffled towards his bedroom to awaken Jerry after giving a curt nod of recognition to Vivian.

"Estelle, is everything going well with y'all?" Vivian rushed up to me, giving me a quick hug. She pulled back and studied the redness on my face.

"I'm not really sure, ViVi." I closed my eyes to keep collected.

"Well, I brought over some new clothing magazines that my sister got for me, and I wanted to have your opinion on a dress I loved." Vivian drew a roll of magazines from her bag, the pages ruffled from the breeze of riding her bike. She stood a lot taller than I did; her skinny legs seemed to be twice the length of mine. "Can we go to your room to look at them?" She asked with eager.

I grabbed her hand and she followed me through the house towards the living room. As we neared the hallway, Father peeked out of the door. "I'm off to the post office, Estelle." He looked at me with reassurance. "This should only be a few minutes." He glanced behind me at Vivian, "Nice to see you, Vivian." He stumbled past us with Jerry, and headed towards the front door.

"Nice to see you too, Mr. Banks!" She called out after him. I continued to lead her the rest of the way. As we walked into the room, Vivian sat on the couch as she confessed, "Goodness, Estelle, your Father is so kind. I wish mine would treat me like that." She looked off at the ceiling, muttering quickly.

"Oh, well I'll make sure to tell him that. Thank you."

Vivian turned her head back down to give me a bright smile. "Oh! Well, I really need to tell you about this dress." Vivian distracted herself in her magazines and shopping. She pulled out a tattered magazine and flipped to a marked page. A model wore a long red shiny dress, one fit for a bridesmaid or fairytale.

"Wow, ViVi. It sure is pretty." I took a closer look at the dress, taking in all of the beading and fine detail. "Don't you think it might be a little mature for you? And look at the price!" I placed my finger on the corner of the magazine, "$19.00!"

"Oh well, I'll save it for when I become a famous star like Jean Harlow, or Bette Davis!" Vivian giggled and looked out into the distance again, her imagination running wild.

"That would be amazing, ViVi." I took a deep breath, preparing myself. "But, may I ask you for some advice?"

Vivian's head turned back to me, her eyes unfocused. "Hmm?"

"Can I ask for your advice on something?" I asked again, bringing her back into reality.

"Oh, of course Estelle! I just love giving people ideas!" She grinned at me again, her eyes full of excitement.

"Well, I don't know if I need any ideas, ViVi." I laughed quietly at her enthusiasm. "I just need someone to talk with about this."

Vivian swung her legs up onto the couch, sitting on her shins excitely. "Just tell me everything, I want to hear everything." She bounced on the cushion, folding her hair behind her ears.

I began in a weighty tone. "Mother has decided to go up to Boston to live with my Aunt Rose for a while." I watched her, wondering how she was going to respond.

"Whoa, I've always wanted to go up north to a big city! Does she like it there? Is there snow? Does she know anybody famous?"

"Well, no," I revealed to her.

"She should sure go and meet a movie star! Oh, she must be so close to New York City, you should tell her to go there, too!" Vivian seemed as if she was about to explode with excitement.

"I don't know if I can, ViVi." I sucked a corner of my mouth in. "She hasn't been writing back to Father and me."

Vivian's face fell, her bottom lip jutting out. "Oh, dear goodness!" She quickly grabbed my hands, shaking them up and down.

"Father is at the post office attempting to call Aunt Rose. He hopes Mother will be home to answer."

"I sure hope she is too! But what if she's not, what if she's not okay, Estelle! What will you do?" She dropped my hands and bounced off the couch, standing in front of the side table. She began rubbing her fingers on the lampshade, her eyes flickering in all directions of the room.

"Vivian, I am just so worried for her. Father is working almost every day, and I have been taking care of Jerry all summer! It is the summertime, ViVi!" My leg began to shake up and down. "I need Mother to come back ViVi, I really need her, too."

She looked intensely at me. "I mean, why don't you go get her?" She asked as if it was an obvious choice. That idea clicked in my brain, opening up the possibility of getting Mother back.

Father rushed into the living room, "Estelle!" He stopped when he saw me, shaking his head. "There was no response. I'm sorry, honey."

I raised my hands to my ear, blocking out all sound. I sat with my head shaking, eyes closed as the world went still. When I found the confidence to look back around the room, Father and Vivian sat silent, afraid to look at anyone. I looked back at Vivian, nodding at her. She met my eyes and nodded back. Mother needed to come home, and I knew how I was going to get her back. I mouthed silently to Vivian, "Thank you."

4

The silver alarm clock rang, jolting me awake. Reaching over to my bedside table, I turned it off as fast as I could so it wouldn't wake anyone else. It was still dark outside, eerily quiet, and still. I pulled the quilted covers of my bed off me, swinging my legs onto the floor. I clicked the lamp on, my eyes adjusting to the light. I'd prepared my clothes the night before, hanging them up on the doorknob. I took the clothing off the hangers, placing them on the edge of my bed. My room felt humid, condensation building on the windows. I moved the white window curtains to the side, shifting the window open to let in the very early morning air. The single lamp cast shadows across my room making the dresser adjacent to my bed look unusually gloomy. A leather kit bag rested on the floor at the foot of my bed, packed with an extra day of clothing and toiletries.

I took off my yellow, laced nightgown and dressed into a blush pink short-sleeve dress, pressing down the skirt to make sure it fit me just right. I ran a hairbrush through my hair a few times before placing it into the kit bag, and then I lifted the bag onto my bed. Lifting my foot onto the side of the bed, I buckled my Mary Jane shoes. As I looked over my whole room, memories washed over me, making me realize the impact of what I was going to do. Grabbing my bag and turning off the lamp, I crept out of the room as the darkness fell over the floral wallpaper.

The hallway was quiet and gloomy, the floorboards creaking under my feet as I walked. The door to Father's office was directly across the kitchen entryway, but the office was less organized than the kitchen. The office door creaked as I opened it and a musty breeze of air wafting in my face, and the lights flickered on, buzzing as they dimmed. Father's desk sat facing the window, his leather chair patched and dusty. Bookshelves lined the walls, filled with picture frames of past relatives and memorabilia. I dropped my bag on the ground, impatiently walking over to the desk. Leaning over it, I blew clouds of dust away across the surface. I ransacked the drawers, my vision unclear in pale light. My mind started to race, and I began to question my entire decision until I saw it. In the very bottom drawer of Father's desk lay a blue and white stripped shoebox, a ribbon securing it closed. I gently lifted it out of its hiding place, careful not to make a peep. Fiddling the lid off, it fell onto the desktop. Inside was an envelope, and peeking mischievously out of the envelope were about twenty five dollar bills.

I stared at them for an instant before erasing my thoughts and grabbing the envelope. I fastened the shoebox back together, and jammed it back into the desk drawer. I reached across the desk for my kit bag, unzipped it, and stuffed the envelope underneath my folded clothes. Swinging the bag onto my arm, I flipped the light switch back off, the room returned to darkness. I stood outside the door, closing it soundlessly while biting my bottom lip in concentration.

Rushing to the front door, I made sure to keep my footsteps light and my breathing quiet. Passing by the kitchen, I spotted one of Mother's hats, a velvet cap with a rose on it, laying on the windowsill. "She must've left it here in her hurry." I mumbled, walking towards it. Entering the kitchen, I noticed the blue clay bird, Mother's favorite, resting next to her cap. I raised the hat up to my head, barely able to see my reflection in the dark windows. The corner of my lips turned up in a smile as I placed the hat on my head, then turned to head for the door. My feet shuffled on the entryway rug, my heart pounding with determination. I took one last look back at my house, knowing the next time I would be standing in this hallway it would be with Mother, making our family complete again. When I glanced over my old home, my eyes wandered back to the blue bird by the window. I shook my head as I looked at it, the clay bird staring back at me with sad eyes.

"Poor bird," I whispered. "It doesn't have Mother either." My feet carried me back into the kitchen, where I grabbed the clay bird and placed in the pocket of my bag. I finally made it to the front door, and I was ready to leave on my own. I turned the doorknob, every screech it made as loud as a war cry. The door opened to the warm breeze of an early summer morning. My red bike was leaning against the side of the porch, where it always was. The basket, barely big enough to fit a handbag, would now have to carry my large kit bag. I balanced the bike up while I tried to stuff my bag in the basket, odds and ends poking out of every corner. After pushing the bag down for an eternity, it was just sturdy enough so that it wouldn't fall out. I rolled the bike down the porch steps, stopping it just in time so that it didn't gain enough momentum to swerve into the road. I hitched my leg over the bike seat, adjusting myself to get used to the weight of the kit bag added to my bike. Once I was settled, I pushed off the driveway and peddled into the dark streets of Beaufort.

The streets were much calmer in the morning, only a few street lights and houses illuminating my way. I vaguely knew where the train station was, about a thirty-minute bike ride away in a town called Yemassee. I had been there a few times before when Father, Mother, and I would travel. The pavement guiding my way, the quiet night somehow became relaxing. I could see the stars overhead, and wondered if Mother could be seeing the same ones as me all the way up in Boston. The thought sent a shiver down my spine.

After a lengthy trek, I spotted the lighted station in the distance. My tired feet peddled faster. I rode up as close as I could to the station, hopping off where the road ended and the building began. I carried my bike onto a covered platform, tying it to one of the metal poles. I had to use such force to get my big bag from my basket that the momentum knocked me back when it finally released. I walked around the platform, peeling me eyes for an open door to the inside. As I turned the corner, an open area inside the train station revealed itself. There were a few well-used wooden benches, a dirty man asleep atop one of them. Across the room was a counter, with a short balding man sitting on a stool. The man's head was leaned all the way back, his eyes fluttering open and shut, his mouth gaping wide. He wore a little metal badge on his chest that read Ticket Agent. I walked up cautiously to the counter, dropping my back close to my feet.

"Excuse me, Sir?" I inquired, my head tilted to get a better look at him. I took a deep breath, and reached my hand over to shake his shoulder until he awoke. "Excuse me, Sir!" I repeated, this time more urgently. He shuddered awake, looking around himself until he figured out where he was. "Sir?" I tried to look him directly in the eyes, but his were tired and jittery.

"Good morning, young lady." He said in between coughs, sorting advertisement papers on the countertop. "Anything I can help you with?" He looked up from the stack of ads, skeptically looking me over.

"I need to get to Boston. Boston, Massachusetts. Very, very soon, Sir." My voice was fast, now another person knew of my adventure.

He chuckled, "I know where Boston is." His eyes still wavered with suspicion.

"I just need to get there," I told him once more. I bent down to get into my bag, filing through it finding the money. "Sir, I have a way to pay, and this is very urgent."

"I have no doubt that you'll not be robbing me, Sweetie," his posture growing better, his brows becoming increasingly scrunched. "But where are your parents? It would be much safer for you to travel a long distance if you were with them."

My jaw lowered a bit, and I sucked in my lips. I plastered a huge frown on my face. "Oh, Sir, they are both in Boston at the moment. You see, sir, they sent me here to South Carolina to stay with my grandmother, Sir, she is very ill." I looked down at my fingers, dramatically twisting and rubbing them together. I sniffled a few times and then brought the sleeve of my dress over to wipe my nose. "Well, she was anyway, Sir." I pulled out the envelope with the money. "This was her last gift to me, Sir. I want to use it to go back to my home, back to my family in Boston, sir."

His eyes softened, his hand reaching out to pat my shoulder. "Don't worry, young lady, we'll get you back to your family." He stood up and turned around, and then he tore off a piece of paper and stamped it. He pushed it across the counter to me. "Here you go, darling. This'll get you to Charleston; your best bet from there will be going to Raleigh."

My throat filled with confidence, my breathing becoming smoother than it had all morning. I dug in the envelope, but felt the man's warm hand stop me.

"For you, Missy, free of charge." He smiled kindly at me, as if I was a hurt puppy. "The train arrives at five, so you'd better not miss it."

I smiled childishly at him, putting a grin on my face. "Oh, thank you Mr. Ticket Man," I praised him; "you are my hero!"

I picked my bag up with my ticket in hand, ready to find the train.

"And my condolences for your grandmother," He said with a solemn look.

"Oh, it sure is okay." I smiled one last time at him, walking towards the exit.

"Wow, you sure don't got yourself a Yankee accent, you don't!"

I gave him a fake chuckle, then swiftly turned and walked outside. A clock hung from the roof of the station, stating it was ten until five. It was still very dark and grim out, and the morning breeze had begun to pick up. Few people were at the train station; the ones who were there were asleep or about to be. I sat down on a bench, where I was able to look out at the trees and watch them sway in the wind. I looked at some of the people around me, people I had never seen before. I held my bag tight against me, the blue clay bird peering out of the pocket. "We're going to be okay." I told it. The bird sat motionless, its eyes staring straight through me.

I heard a metal screeching, as the train pulled up to the station, and I quickly stood up to be prepared. The big train had many cars with many windows, and it looked like many seats. I pulled out my ticket, finding my car and seat. Car four, seat eleven. I walked the length of the train, up to the front, where the conductor had gone and put a portable wooden staircase to walk up. As I began to go up, he held out his hand to help me. "Here you are, Miss." He smiled a much calmer smile then the one from the ticket agent. "Ticket, please?" He accepted the ticket and examined it, then returned it and pointed to his left. "Miss, you are four cars down, second row, middle seat on right." His voice was strong and deep, and he dismissed me with a nod.

My bag, the clay bird, and I were all ready to go on our adventure. I walked through three train cars until I got to one with a door that said car four. "Second row on the right, second row on the right," I mumbled to myself. The rest of the people on the train were asleep, had a hat covering their eyes, or they were reading books or newspapers. I saw my row, the second row, full except for the middle seat on the right. I squeezed in between two older men, both asleep, and placed my kit bag under the seat.

"Everybody, tickets out!" The conductor's loud voice boomed, approaching from the very front of the car. He came by and punched a hole in our tickets with a swiftness I had never seen before. The conductor finished with my car and walked into the next one. The train rumbled and whistled, taking off for Charleston.

5

The train tumbled to a stop amid a crashing of noises as people gathered their stuff. Throughout the trip, the train's force had pushed my bag further and further underneath my seat. While the other passengers began walking out of the car, I pursued my luggage. I launched myself onto the floor of the train, the man next to me staring. I shoved my head down to spot the bag, and saw the handle had caught on a sharp edge of the seat. I yanked, pulled, and tugged at the strap, until I heard a disturbing rip come from under the seat. I resurfaced with my bag; the man seated next to me, had eyes wide. One of my kit bag handles now had only a single side attached.

"Well, of course." He snickered, folding up some papers and placing them into his coat pocket. I gave him an awkward laugh while I stood back up. The bag had become unwieldy to carry, I now had to hold it up from the underside.

A long line had formed at the end of the car, people standing, staring at the floor, waiting to get off. I took a last look around the train, taking in some of the details I had never noticed before. Finely carved wood paneling surrounding the ceiling, and a few of the windows were open. I reached the top of the line, and stepped down the metal staircase with my heart on fire with excitement. My feet, sore from sitting down for so long, hit the gravel road, and I was on my way. Swarms of people were crowded around me, and everyone looked so different. I followed the course of movement, joining the people who walked into a very large building. A young boy stood next to me, wearing a little grey vest and hat. He held hands with who was presumably his mother, hurrying him along through the rush of people. People sure are in a hurry in the big city! I came into an immense domed room, with counters full of workers in the middle, and gates on every side. Bells were going off in every direction, people sprinting towards them on the marble floor. Others were sitting on benches, reading newspapers or examining train tickets. I wandered around in wonder, my breath catching at the disorder around me. Two sizeable glass doors opened, busy people hustling though them; men with briefcases leaving, women carrying children entering. I squeezed my way through them, shoulder to shoulder with strangers I had never met. Every-thing smelled of cigarettes and sweat. Escaping the enormous train station, my feet hit the sidewalk. My bag had broken, my stomach was rumbling, and I had arrived in a new city alone; no one knew where I was.

It was evening in Boston, and big shiny lights materialized from the tall buildings above. I came across an empty bench positioned underneath a street lamp. Placing my bag on the bench, I sat down with a sigh. I stared at my hands, my eyelids heavy, and I felt disoriented. I reached inside my broken bag, fiddling around for the letter. I pulled the envelope out, taking note of the return address. Mother kept her mail in a drawer by the kitchen, and this letter was from Aunt Rose. Her address was sprawled in elegant writing on the back corner. "Where could this be?" I whispered to myself, covering my ears with my hands and setting my elbows in my lap. My leg bounced on the cement. My eyes circled back and forth across the street, cars lined up, and people walked in between them.

It was crowded and foggy, the sun setting and casting a golden hue over the city. A cluster of businessmen stood on the edge of the curb waiting to cross the street. I stood up, closed my bag and clutched the letter in my hand. My bag had made my arms sore, and even carrying it a few paces was tiring. I collected myself and stood behind the cluster, following them until they crossed the street. The road was large and intimidating, cars honking and jammed. I quickened my pace, the dark pavement beneath me felt rough. I arrived at the curb, a bookstore lit up in front of me. A grey stone building loomed over the store, bearing a thousand windows. I began walking down the sidewalk, passing newspaper boys and beggars. "Joe Louis knocks out Germany's Max Schmeling! Get the story here!" A young paperboy hollered while hawking a stack of newspapers. Two women were yelling at each other on opposite sides of the concrete, their faces red and eyes puffy. I rushed in between them, my head down, not looking.

Down the street, wooden stands were set out holding great containers of fruit and bread. As I came closer, I noticed the immense number of items for sale. There were weaved baskets full of bananas, across from them buckets stacked full of tomatoes. Clusters of green and purple grapes hung from a wooden stand, and market goers walked with their bags full. A sea of heads of lettuce piled up into a human sized tub. Aisles formed in between these containers, people waiting in line to grab a handful of carrots or blueberries. I made my way into a section of fresh bread, and I looked over all of the options. Signs with scribbles letters read "Sourdough" or "Baguette." I picked up a slice of a warm baguette from the tray, and folded it into a napkin. From the fruit section, I grabbed two peaches, and held them atop the bread. I started towards what appeared to be a line for a register when I heard feet shuffle behind me.

"You need help finding something?" a thick Boston accent inquired from behind me. I turned to locate who was speaking to me. A tall boy with dark chocolate hair was facing me. He had on a light beige shirt and wrinkled navy blue pants that needed pressing.

"Oh, no." I respond to him. "I just needed these." I held up the stack of bread and peaches I had gathered.

"Lucky you found some nice peaches," he told me. "Most of the ones we've been getting lately have been mushy." He sighed and glanced at the large basket of peaches.

I wondered why he wanted to assist me, I asked. "So, you work here?"

He nodded, "Sure do." He pointed his chin towards the girl working at the cash register. "Over there, that's my sister. We're family owned."

I laughed quietly and smiled in her direction. "I guess I'll go over there to pay, then." I told him, turning back.

"Aye, I'll walk you over there, you'll be able to skip the line." He strutted in front of me, wanting me to follow him. We made our way over to the stand with the register, small bouquets of flowers for sale behind it. He spun around, his hands out towards me. "Pass 'em to me." He whispered. I placed the food in his hands, and he took it. He left swiftly, leaving me alone next to the line. In the line, an older woman raised her eyebrows at me, looking me over. She gave me a critical smile, sucking her cheeks in.

I stood up on my tiptoes, watching above the line as he bent behind the stand. He appeared behind the register, next to the girl he said was his sister. She had straight brown hair, and was tall like him. He bent his head to her ear, showing her the bread and peaches I had handed him. He said something quietly to her, his eyes finding me across the group of people that were waiting. Her eyes followed his, setting on me. He looked to be asking her a question, and then glanced at the register. She nodded, her lips pressed in her mouth and her head tilted to the side. He mouthed, "Thank you so much." She looked back at me, and then carried on with the cash register. He weaved his way in between everyone, still carrying my food. He reached me, holding the peaches and bread out in front of him.

"These are for you." He extended the food, now wrapped in brown paper and inside a bag, as he moved even closer to me. I took it, but kept my eyes on him. "No, sorry, I haven't paid yet." My mouth stayed opened, was I being impolite?

"You don't have to."

"No, no. I can pay for it. I have money," I went to open my bag, balancing it on my knees, as my hands were full. Standing on one foot, my leg wobbled but I fetched the envelope with money out. His eyes expanded as his sucked in a breath.

"You're carrying around all of that?" He exclaimed, his voice loud.

I needed him to quiet down. "I've just been traveling," I smiled to ease him. "I made it all the way from South Carolina."

"So you brought all that? Where you staying, a castle?" He was still caught up on the envelope of money.

His joke made me giggle. "I'm staying with my aunt." I responded. "But, she doesn't know that I am."

"How does she not know, you're her niece, right?" He talked with his hands, and looked around as if he was speaking to an audience. "What's her name, maybe I know her." He paused. "She come to the market a lot?"

"I really don't know if she does." I shook my head. "Her name is Rose Ward."

He tilted his head and looked at me, "And what's your name?"

"Estelle."

"Whoa, like a star? That French or something?" He snickered. "Rose, Rose." He continued, "Yeah, I don't know of any Roses. You know where she lives?"

I pulled out the letter with her return address and handed it to him.

"Wherever that is."

He looks over the letter, analyzing the sophisticated handwriting. "This is a few blocks down, maybe ten, or fifteen."

"Oh that's great. Thank you so much... uh," not knowing his name, I just stared.

He laughed and glanced at his feet. "Raymond."

"Well, thank you Raymond, for the food and the directions." I turned away from him, my bag in one hand, and the food in another.

"Maybe I'll see you later!" He called after me as I started to walk back down the sidewalk.

"Yeah, maybe!" I called back at him, but kept walking.

I managed to walk only half a block before I heard the same footsteps behind me.

"Estelle!" Only one person in Boston knew my name. I stopped in my tracks. "You're not here with anyone, are you?" He ran to catch up with me, and then began walking next to me.

"You sure ask a lot of questions." I teased. "I'm not."

Raymond jogged to advance in front of me. Turning around, he faced me and walked backwards down the sidewalk. "How 'bout I walk you there? To your aunt's house?" He asked with a smile. He raised his arms, spanning them out on either side of him.

I sighed a breath of relief. "That would be so helpful."

We walked down the sidewalk a little more, passing by even more huge buildings with bright signs. "ViVi would love this place." I told myself.

"Huh?" Raymond questioned. I almost forgot he was there.

"My friend ViVi, from back home. She's always wanted to go to a big city like this." I smiled at ViVi, remembering the last time I saw her and how she told me about her dreams of being famous in a big city.

"So, you got friends back home." He remarked. "Then why are you here, staying with an aunt who… doesn't know you are?"

"It's a long story, Raymond." I told him.

"Aye, we got a little more to walk. I can listen."

"If you really want to." We continued down the dark street, passing alleyways where rats scampered as they heard our footsteps. "My mother just had a baby. His name is Jerry." My eyes glanced at him, but continued to look straight ahead.

"What's wrong with him?" He asked, fixing his hair.

My eyes opened wide, and a hearty laugh escaped from my throat. "Nothing's wrong with him. He's my brother!" I continued to laugh, thinking about his question.

He smiled as well, "I mean, something must be! Why else would you move across the country?"

"Oh, no. It's just me." I told him secretively.

"Only you!" He declared, "You're moving by yourself?"

My eyes shut as I giggled, "I'm not moving here, Raymond. I ran away."

"Didn't know I'd get caught up with a runaway today, Estelle." He was fully laughing now. His cheeks were turning red, and he stopped on the sidewalk to calm down.

I had to take a deep breath. "I am not a runaway!" I told him through gasping laughs.

"You told me you ran away. If you ran away, you're a runaway!" He shrugged the side of his shoulder into mine was we strolled.

"My mother is here. I came to see her. My father doesn't know I left."

"He probably knows you did now."

Raymond was right. As we followed the sidewalk and left the center of downtown, I began to think about Father and Jerry. Father would have to take care of him full time now. "He's probably worried, but I'll write him a letter when I get to my aunt's."

"He's where you got your money from, right?" He urged. He positioned his hands in his pockets, speeding up his pace. My face felt hot, and the silence on the street was loud. A breeze began to pick up, swarming the warm air through his hair. The wind made mine tangle, and I jerked my head to get it out of my eyes. He and I carried on walking, and I quickened my stride to keep up with his.

"So, I'm making pals with a runaway and a stealer." He chuckled but his joke didn't help. "Ah, don't worry. I won't tell anyone. Don't even know who I would." I stopped staring at the ground, and gave him a tired smile. I followed Raymond as he turned the street corner, and he stopped in front of a large white house. It had a grand porch with tall steps, and was at least three floors high. Its walls attached to the houses on either side of it, but the size of Aunt Rose's was immense.

"This should be your place."

Sure enough, the address on the letter matched the house. "Thank you, again." I told him.

"Always."

I hoisted my belonging up Aunt Rose's staircase. When I reached the top, I turned to watch Raymond walk away.

"Nice to meet you!" I called my voice shaky.

"Good night, Estelle." He replied, roaming back down the dim sidewalk.

The lights in Aunt Rose's house were dark, and there seemed to be no movement inside. A gold-plated doorbell was affixed on the door case. I pressed my fingers against it, praying someone would answer. The breezy air turned from warm to cool, and the shadows cast across the porch. After a few seconds of silence, I decided to try the door knocker. It matched the doorbell, gold and shiny. I knocked three times, the door knocker sure to wake someone up. Still, there was no answer. I tried the bell and knocker each once more, until a lock turned from the other side the door. A key clanged inside the lock, and a chain lock hit the wooden door. It cracked open, a set of brown eyes peering out at me. I quickly picked my bags back up, and readjusted my posture.

"Who are you?" The lady asked. She was wearing a silk night gown and slippers, her hair done up in rolls.

"Hello, ma'am. My name is Estelle Banks, I'm looking for Miss Rose Ward?"

The woman's mouth dropped. Her face was strained, her eyes losing any ounce of tiredness they had before. "And your need to visit her at this hour is?" Her voice was monotone, her eyebrows raised.

"I'm so sorry to disturb you, but I'm her niece. My mother, Mary Banks is here as well. I thought Aunt Rose and my mother would let me stay."

"Rose is not here. I am deeply sorry." She spoke fast and deliberately, moving to close the door. I stuck my hand out, stopping her.

"Ma'am, my mother, she must be here." I told her, fear boiled in my mind and my head became light.

Wrinkles appeared on her forehead, her expression shocked. "You must have the wrong address, child. I do not know of a Mary Banks." She pushed the door harder, closing it with a slam.

I reached for the door knocker, ramming it into the door.

"Excuse me!" I shouted, hoping the lady could hear me. "Please, I need to see my mother!" I screamed louder. Panic filled me, my throat catching whenever I inhaled. There was still no answer. I moved away from the door, near a rocking chair on the porch. I sat down, my body heavy and tired from the long travel. I took out my only other dress, laying it across my lap as a blanket. I jammed my bag between my neck and the chair, resting on it like a pillow.

Periodically, I turned to the door in case she would answer again, but no response came. I rocked in the chair, the wind growing stronger and whistling in the night breeze. I picked at my pulled together dinner, the bread now a little hard and the peaches warm. This has to be Aunt Rose's house. *Where could my mother be?*

"At least I've found a friend here." I whispered to myself, picking at my fingernails. My head became heavy, and I drifted to sleep while watching the shadowy, dark, Boston road.

I stirred awake, my eyes foggy and confused. Cars were honking down the street, people passed Aunt Rose's house in suits and dresses, some walking dogs and others carrying briefcases. The sun was bright, the porch ceiling providing me shade. I could see the house more clearly now, white details on the window sills and carvings in the hand railings. I pushed myself up from the rocking chair, and my extra dress fell to the ground. I knelt to fold it back up, laying it in the bottom of my bag. The broken handle with the bulky bag now very impractical. I set it by my feet as I faced the front door once more. I used the knocker with even more force than I had the previous night, making a dent in the door's paint. While I stood by, waiting for an answer, I noticed my hair in the window reflection. Using my bag as a pillow was mildly comfortable, but did not serve a good purpose to my hair. I haphazardly smoothed it down with my hands, getting my fingers caught in a few small knots. After no acknowledgement from inside the house, I gathered my belongings and made my way back down the staircase. Turning right, I tried to follow the same path Raymond led me last night, guessing at every turn. A sturdy plump man with a large hat kept pace behind me, holding a briefcase, on his way to work.

With my stomach grumbling and my throat dry, I reached the market again. The bright sun reflected off some of the fruit, and warmed the bread. Making my way through the aisle, I picked up a second slice of baguette, and got a single apple. Taking in my surroundings in the daylight, the city was intriguing. More people were walking about the market than the night before. Families roamed through the sidewalk, small children grabbing candied plums and flowers. Beyond the row of fruit cases, stood a figure with the same dark brown hair that I knew the day before. This time he was wearing a light blue shirt and beige pants, opposite of yesterday. I walked up beside him, my bag still in my sore hand. "Good morning."

He whirled around, setting a container of broccoli on a case of supplies. "Estelle, you're back!" He looked down at the collection of food I held. "That all you're getting this morning?"

I handed the apple and the bread slice to him. "Definitely. But I'm paying this time." I held my leg up again, balancing my bag on my thigh. I dug my hand around, fishing for the envelope. I pulled it out, presenting it to Raymond. I moved too briskly, and the contents of the bag spilled onto the pavement. I gasped, "I am so sorry." I apologized to him, as he watched me pick everything back up.

"Oh-oh," he exclaimed. He stood there awkwardly, reaching to help after I had everything back inside the bag. "Don't apologize, everything's fine."

I stuffed the blue clay bird into the bag as I said, "It only just broke yesterday, on the train here." I stood back up, with the bag in-between my armss.

"I've seen birds like that in souvenir shops before, you travel?" He asked me, gesturing to the bag with the bird.

"Oh, no. It's my mother's."

"You staying with her and your aunt, right?"

"Planning too." I motioned to my dress, the same one I had on yesterday. "I wasn't able to get in last night."

"Aye, that's strange. Where'd you sleep for the night?"

I began to answer him, when a familiar man strutted up to us. He was shorter than Raymond, and more round than him, too. He wore the same flimsy hat as the man behind me this morning, and carried a similar briefcase.

"Estelle Banks." His voice was directed harshly at me.

I glanced up at Raymond, shocked that this stranger knew my name. I tilted my head in question, and Raymond shrugged his shoulders at me.

"Sir?" I told him, inching backwards.

He took his hat off, holding it next to his bulky briefcase. He cleared his throat aggressively, setting his eyes severely onto me.

"I've been asked to give you a warning." His voice was strong, he was almost shouting at me.

"Why'd you need a warning?" Raymond asked, his faced scrunched up, confused and almost amused.

"A warning?" I questioned the man, "What have I done?" I shook my head, tilting it towards Raymond. "I don't have any idea, I've been here less than a day." I whispered to him.

"Ms. Banks, Rose Ward reported that you harassed her last night, and illegally trespassed on her property." I let out a fast breath. "If you trespass again, the police will be called, and you could face arrest."

I stuck my neck out towards him in bewilderment, and shuffled back behind Raymond.

"Ha! Arrest!" Raymond bellowed, a crazy grin on his face. "You must be fooling us!" He stepped towards him, his head glancing back at me. "Who is this man?"

I shrugged my shoulders.

"You will call me Mr. King." The man demanded at him.

"Of course, Mr. King." He responded sarcastically, giving the man a joking curtsy.

"And who has she been, you said, harassing? She's been in town less than a day!"

Mr. King thrusted his chubby fist into Raymond's shoulder. "Young man, quit your threatening behavior, or the police will be called."

Raymond's mouth hung open, any indication of past amusement in his face gone. "Police? You can't be serious!"

Mr. King ignored Raymond, and twisted his irregular body past him, rambling closer to me. "This will be your last warning, Ms. Banks. Have a good day." He was an inch away from me, and placed his hat back on without breaking his intimidating eye contact. He sauntered away, a few market goers who saw the scene watching.

Raymond stood watching closely as he waked away, then turned dramatically back to me. "What was that?" His voice was loud and exasperated. He came closer to me, looking around before he whispered, "How many more criminal things can you do, Runaway?"

My eyes had gathered tears, and my bag had become too heavy to hold. I set it on the ground in front of my feet, bringing my hands to cover my face. "I don't know what to do, Raymond."

"What have you gotten into, Estelle?" It seemed like his shock was wearing off, and he was now gaining interest.

"I haven't done anything!" I sucked my lips in to keep from crying. "After you left last night, I knocked on the door for such a long time! No one answered for quite a while, until I woke up a woman inside and she told me to leave!" My breathing became fast, my face pale.

"And this lady was your aunt?" He asked, gears shifting in his mind.

I shrugged my shoulders and looked up to the sky. There wasn't a cloud anywhere, and I could see tears begin to well again. I gasped. "She had brown eyes like Mother, and it was her address. She had to have been, right? I mean, she must've!" My voice broke. "I don't know what to do, I don't know if my mother is in that house or not. I don't know anything!"

"How 'bout you breathe, and eat the apple. You really don't have to pay this time."

I sat down onto my bag, tired and filthy and confused. "I'm so sorry I brought this to you, Raymond."

He knelt down on the ground next to me, handing me the apple. He stood back up, looking around and down the street. Even with the current circumstances, a little smirk grew on his face. "Don't worry 'bout it." He bounced to his feet, his eyes full of ideas. He smiled at me, the foolishness in his expression returned. "This'll give me something to do."

His eagerness earned a laugh.

6

The marketplace became livelier with more customers flowing into the aisles. Raymond stood above me, glancing back and forth from around the market to me.

He cleared his throat, "Maybe this aunt of yours mistook you for someone else." He frowned.

I stood up from my bag, feeling dizzy. "He knew me, he knew my aunt!" My tone definitely heated. "I don't think it was a mistake!" I shook my hair out of my face, shaking my hands by my sides.

"Do you think you're gonna go back there, maybe try again?" He mumbled, not sure if he should be asking me that question.

I threw my head back, becoming more and more flustered, "No! Why would I try that? I don't have any idea where my Mother is, and my aunt sent someone after me! Now I have no place to stay, so why would I go back there? Just so she can call the police to arrest me? I'm in this place where people talk so strangely, and my only friend is you!" My heart beat faster, my head felt lighter. My feet were bouncing up and down on the pavement, and I clutched my hand over my mouth.

Raymond's eyebrows shot up, and he side-eyed the food he was holding, the food that he let me have free.

My shoulders dropped and I slowed my voice. "I didn't mean to offend you, Raymond." I apologized.

"I'm not offended, Estelle. I'm more concerned for you!" He chuckled nervously, attempting to lighten the mood.

I sighed. "My family at home must be worried sick! Oh, why did I come here?"

Raymond stood with his mouth open, and his brows furrowed. "I have a suggestion, it might make this better. Okay?"

I knelt down to grab my bag, holding it up by my shoulders. I turned to look at him. "What?"

He made a fist against his mouth. "What if," he moved his hand out in front of him, "you," he used both hands to gesture towards me, "stayed with my family." He pointed his fingertips to his chest.

I exhaled and rolled my eyes, turning away from him. "I can't. I won't burden you or your family."

"My family is big enough, people stay in often, and you need somewhere to stay the night." He seemed sincere, "We've let in more guests than I can count. You will not be a burden." He chuckled.

I took a deep breathe, realizing he really meant it. I still questioned him. "How far is it?" I bent down to collect my bag.

His eyes lit up, "Just a few blocks, don't worry." I titled my head. "How about you come have lunch there, and decide for yourself, deal?" He stuck out his hand.

I nodded my head and shook his hand, "Deal."

We made our way out of the market, the crowd of people dwindled as we got further away. The streets of Boston were loud and booming, cars honking at each other and people chatting as they crossed the streets. Tall grey buildings loomed overhead, almost touching the sky. Policemen guarded the entrances, wearing long blue dress uniforms and shiny hats. Each officer wore a serious expression, staring blankly into the street.

"Are they always that dull?" I asked Raymond.

He startled, as if he was in deep thought while we were walking. "Who?"

I jerked my chin towards them and whispered, "The police men."

He shrugged his shoulders, "Those cops got nothing to be happy about."

"Oh."

We continued down the street, and came across light posts with chewed bubble gum attached and newspapers discarded by the curb. A skinny stray dog trotted in between Raymond and me, and began to bark at a pecking pigeon.

"That poor dog," I frowned. "Why doesn't anyone feed it?"

He glanced over his shoulder to look back at it. "Nobody owns it."

"Nobody wants it?" I asked, worried.

"That things probably got rabies." He laughed to himself, waiting for me to become amused as well. His joke wasn't funny.

He grew quiet, his cheeks grew red as he watched his feet. "Sorry."

"For what?"

"I guess you're an animal lover?" He looked back up at me.

I shook my head. "It just looked so malnourished. It makes my skin crawl."

He nodded quickly, trying to show me he agreed.

We proceeded under an awning, and I peered through two glimmering glass double doors. A golden plaque beside them read *Omni Parker House Hotel.* A tall woman, wearing an ankle-length fur coat made her way inside, two bellboys silently holding the doors for her. A man in a suit followed her, holding the hand of a small girl. The girl had on a skirt and a knit sweater, with red ribbons tied in bows around her braids. She carried a small stuffed rabbit, and tugged at the man's hand. Behind the family, two hotel workers loaded their load of luggage onto a dolly. Their luggage followed closely behind them, and they all disappeared behind the hotel doors.

"Wealthy people," Raymond pointed them out. He joked, "Maybe they know your aunt."

We turned the corner after we passed the hotel, a cool breeze wafting by us. Sitting against a brick building was a small old woman, wrapped in a filthy green blanket with no shoes. A tin can sat in front of her, a few pennies lying inside. The women's face and arms were skinny and wrinkled, her grey hair falling past her elbows.

I left Raymond and knelt in front of her. "How are you, ma'am?" I asked, her eyes half shut and unfocused.

Looking past me, she stuck her hand out and pointed at the tin can. "Over there." Her voice was raspy and slow, and I could see her few teeth had turned yellow and brown.

I nodded, "Oh, of course." I picked myself back up and made my way to the can. I fumbled through my bag, reaching for the envelope of money.

Raymond grabbed my arm to stop me. "What are you doing?" He whispered. His eyes were wide and he looked at me with disbelief.

"That poor woman needs help!" I whisper shouted back, jerking my head in her direction. The woman looked unfazed, and she was staring off into the street behind us.

"Don't give beggars money, Estelle." He grabbed my bag in one hand and tugged at my arm to lead me in the other direction. I tried to get him to let go of me, but he wouldn't. "They all just sit there and rot until they scam enough generous people into giving them free money." He was very adamant.

"An old woman shouldn't have to sit there and starve, Raymond! Not while rich families with their expensive, unwrinkled clothes, get to trot right past her into a golden hotel!"

He rolled his eyes. "If she wanted to get help, she could ask the police where the nearest soup kitchen is."

I yanked my arm out of his grip. "I can't believe you wouldn't help her!" I snapped. "Try to be more generous." I began to walk in front of him.

"Hey, I'm letting a stranger into my house because she doesn't have anywhere to stay! I think that's being extremely generous."

"And you wouldn't let me give a stranger a donation." I started to walk faster.

Raymond called from behind me, "You know where you're going?"

I thought I could hear a laugh.

"Oh, don't be a know it all. I can take care of myself." I stopped abruptly in front of the street, an intersection ahead of me. Crowds of people gathered by the crosswalks, and made their way across the street in a cluster as soon as the cars slowed down. I looked down the street both directions, examining the paths I could take. I continued straight, and joined the line crossing the street.

"Nope."

I exhaled, becoming increasingly annoyed. I turned around to face him dramatically.

"We're turning right, right here." He smiled.

"Fine."

He led the rest of the way until we arrived at his house. It was part of a red brick building with a single back door. We walked up a set of skinny stairs to make it to the small front porch.

"Houses here look very different." I commented, becoming aware of the style of the buildings surrounding me.

"Different how?" He replied.

"Shape, material, height." I told him. "Buildings here are a lot taller and skinnier."

He questioned me, "Well what does your house look like?" Raymond twisted the metal door handle and propped the door open with his knee, gesturing for me to go inside.

"My house is flat, only one floor. And all my neighbors and I have wood on the outside, not brick."

The front door led directly into the kitchen, which shared space with the living room. A slender staircase in the corner of the room turned to a hallway upstairs. The room lights were all out, except for some light coming from under a door in the back of the kitchen. Raymond flipped a few switches, and the lights flickered on.

"Is anyone else home?" I asked him, looking around the small first floor.

He looked towards the door to the room with the lights on, "My sister, probably."

I took a seat at the kitchen table. "So your whole family works at the market?"

"Sure do."

"You're parents are there right now?" I asked.

"I'm sure my dad is picking up shipments, he usually does every Wednesday." He opened the cupboard and pulled a box out. "Want any Wheat Krispies?"

"For lunch?"

"Why not?" He pulled out two bowls and set them on the table. He tipped the cardboard cereal over the bowls, and began to pour. A loud banging on the front door startled him and the Wheat Krispies spilled all over the table in front of me.

"Oh, I am so sorry, Estelle!" He apologized, and I picked some cereal bits off my dress and placed them on a napkin.

"Raymond!" A girl's voice yelled from behind the front door. "Ray, you home?"

I stood from the chair, scooping the Wheat Krispies into a pile. Raymond made his way across the kitchen to the front door. He swung the door open, and standing there was a short girl with big puffy brown hair. It seemed she had tried to cut her hair into bangs, but tight curls fell into her brown eyes anyways.

"Raymond, I have to tell you…," she stopped when she looked behind him at me. She directed her attention to me, "who's this?"

"That's Estelle." He backed up from the door, letting her in.

She made her way past him. "My name's Della."

I stuck my hand out, "Oh, nice to meet you, I'm Estelle."

"You talk funny, where you from?" She asked, forgetting to shake my hand.

"South Carolina." Raymond responded for me. "She's gonna stay here for a little bit."

I walked closer to the two of them. I corrected him, "Only one night."

"Whoa, you'd rather stay here than with your family?" She laughed. "Nice choice."

Raymond pipped in, "She doesn't have a choice, Della. She has a problem."

She acted surprised, "They kick you out or something?"

"Not really."

"They did, sent the police after her and everything." He told her.

I gasped, "It was not the police, Raymond!"

"They sent a creep after her. He threatened us this morning."

Della began to walk further into the house, grabbing a handful of cereal out of the box that Raymond was still holding.

"A threat? What are you guys planning to do?"

"Not sure yet," he said. "For right now, Estelle's here."

Della frowned, "Anything you want me to do for you?"

I looked at Raymond, shrugging my shoulders.

"Estelle, Della's mom is a nurse."

"Oh?"

"She is." Della stated. "What's the big deal about that?"

Raymond started smiling. "Is she at work right now?"

Della nodded at him as if he was dumb.

Raymond announced, "I've got an idea."

7

Della stood with her hands on her hips, "What, Raymond?" She rolled her eyes. She leaned over next to me, pointing at him and said, "He's a bonehead."

"I heard that when people go missing, they show up at hospitals." Raymond tried to get his point across to us.

Della stared at him blankly, expecting him to continue. "Her mother is missing?"

"She told our family she would be in Boston with my Aunt, she's not. My Aunt was the one that sent that man after me."

"Crap, man."

Raymond stepped closer to us, waving his hands around, "Della, your mother is a nurse; a nurse at a hospital."

"Would she be at the hospital, you think?" I asked him. "Do you think she's hurt?"

Della's eyes grew wide, her mouth dropping a bit. She piped in, "He may be right. They hold records there, is it possible she could've gotten sick, or gone in for an appointment?"

"I hadn't thought about that– possibly." I began to feel worried, my stomach turning. "Do y'all think she could've gotten sick?"

Della's face turned soft, "They might have records of her. Don't worry."

"How about we ask your Mother, she might be able to check." Raymond proposed. "She has access to files right?"

"She does, but she wouldn't listen to us. We would need an adult to ask." Della was still standing in the doorway, but she began to back up. The ground floor of Raymond's home was dense, the kitchen table backed up into the corner of the house with the many chairs crowded around.

"Della, would your Mother trust Raymond's Mother? Could we get her to ask for information?" She shrugged her shoulders. "She's really protective over her work. We would have to really convince her."

Raymond shoved his hand into the box of cereal he was still holding, and ate another handful. "What if we get my Mom to invite her over for tea tonight? Then we'll tell her Estelle's predicament, then, *boom*," He clapped his hands, "we'll know where Estelle's mother is."

"I'll talk to her when she gets off of work tonight, how about that?" Della smirked. "She's really difficult to persuade, but I'll try my best."

"So you'll do it?" Raymond asked her, smiling.

Della laughed. "For Estelle, but don't get your hopes up."

I gave Della a shaky smile. "Thank you. So, we have a plan?"

I looked between them, Raymond chewing on cereal straight out of the box, Della standing in the doorway confidently.

Della nodded, "I'll ask her tonight, but no guarantee she'll come over here."

"*When* she comes over, and agrees to talk, we'll figure out what to do next." Raymond insisted.

The three of us stood in silence, Della picking at her fingernails. "I better go," she told us.

"See you guys tonight." Raymond's eyes lit up, and he glanced at me.

"Hopefully." She added, smiling. She walked back towards the door, but before she got a chance to get her hand on the doorknob, the door jerked open.

A women with wavy black hair walked in, bags of groceries in her arms. She wore glasses and a black coat, even though it was warm outside. She dropped the bags on the tabletop, and began to pull out the contents of them.

"Mrs. Collins!" Della gushed.

The woman stopped unloading the groceries and turned around. When she laid eyes on Della, an excited grin grew on her face. "Della Davis!" The woman exclaimed, "I haven't seen you in forever!" She walked over to give her a big hug. The two of them rocked back and forth, squeezing each other tight. When she finally let go she asked, "How is your summer going, darling?"

"It's been good. Boring, but good." Della answered.

"I like to hear that." She gave her a pat on the shoulder.

Della directed her attention back to me, "I'll see you later, Estelle."

I gave her a small wave as she walked out of Raymond's house, her dark brown curls blowing in the wind.

The women turned to look at Raymond, and looked surprised when she saw me.

"Who is this?" She asked Raymond.

I spoke up, "My name is Estelle Banks," I told her, sticking out my hand for her to shake.

"Well, nice to meet you, Estelle. I'm Mrs. Collins, Raymond's mom." She grabbed my hand with both of hers and squeezed it tight. "I hear something in your voice, where you from?"

"South Carolina." I told her.

"What are you doing all the way up here?" She exclaimed. She shook off her coat.

Raymond grabbed the coat from her. "It's a long story." He placed her coat on the rack by the front door.

"I'm here to find my mother." I told her. "She took a train up here a few weeks ago, but we haven't heard from her since."

Mrs. Collins placed her hand on the table behind her, leaning back and listening to me closely. "And I assume your father is here with you, dear?" She pursed her lips.

"Oh, no ma'am." I choked out. I began to continue with my explanation but Raymond interrupted.

"She traveled here alone." He offered up my information.

His mother's eyebrows shot up like a bullet, her mouth falling open. She swayed slightly into the table chair, causing it to make a screech.

Raymond stood frozen, and I saw him try to keep a smile from his face while he watched his mother's disbelief. "On a train." He added.

Mrs. Collins, blinking slowly between her son and me, reclaimed her balance and stood up straight. "Well, that is," she took in a deep breath, "brave." She squeezed the wooden chair behind her, her knuckles turning white.

"And your mother?" She could barely get the words out of her mouth.

I bit my lip, contemplating the best way to tell an adult of my journey. "I don't know where she's gone. She told my father and me that she would be staying with my aunt, but she's not."

She put her hand over her chest, her tone quickly switching from shock to sympathy. "I am so sorry, darling." She pouted her lips.

I shook my head and inhaled. "No, no. Everything's fine. I was just speaking to Raymond and Della about checking the hospitals for her tomorrow." I tried to give her a small smile of reassurance; I didn't want an adult to worry for me.

"The hospitals?" She looked over to her son. "Where did you get that idea?" She crossed her arms in front of her.

He slouched, "I was hoping we could ask Nurse Davis?" He stared at her.

Mrs. Collins let out a sharp laugh, and turned around to face the grocery bags. "If you think that Kay will let three children into the hospital to find a missing woman, you need to use your head more, Raymond."

I leaned towards Raymond, my eyebrows pinched towards his mother.

"Kay is Della's mother." He whispered.

I gave him a slow nod and turned my attention back to Mrs. Collins. She began to take ingredients out of the bag aggressively, haphazardly organizing them on the tabletop.

"Estelle, right?" She continued to look away from me and focus on the groceries.

"Yes, ma'am."

"You said she was going to live with your aunt?" She stopped and looked over her shoulder, waiting for my response.

I nodded my head quickly. "Mhm."

"Your aunt, in Boston?"

"Yes." I told her. "Boston. Here." I could feel my eyes opening wider, and I resumed nodding my head.

"Dear, have you checked with her? Your mother did say she would be staying with her, right? I assume you're staying with your aunt as well, yes?"

"Oh, no ma'am. Raymond actually showed me to her house last night, but she wasn't there. I was thinking of trying again today but while I was at the market a man had followed—"

"Her mother wasn't there, Ma!" Raymond exclaimed. He stepped on my foot, interrupting me. He was smiling at his mother, his eyes wide and crazy.

Mrs. Collins raised her eyebrows at him, leaning back on the chair, observing his suspicious behavior.

"We went back to the market to see if maybe her mother had stumbled upon it to get something to eat." He gave his head a quick tilt, "Right, Estelle?" He turned towards me dramatically, using his foot to put more pressure on mine.

I sucked in breath, realizing what he meant. "Mhmm." I told her, trying to grin wide.

"Well then," She squinted at her son. "If you need to speak to Nurse Davis, we can try to arrange that." She grabbed her load of groceries and took them to the sink.

Raymond and I were now behind her, and he spun in my direction. "Thank you." He mouthed.

"Sure." I uttered.

"Now, Estelle," Mrs. Collins called. Her suddenly loud tone startled me. "Where have you been staying?"

I looked at Raymond; he shook his head while shrugging his shoulders.

"I slept on my aunt's porch last night." I mumbled.

She heard me. "Good Lord!" She cried. "Are you feeling well? You slept outside the whole night, in this city?" Her face had turned pale. "Well, you can always stay here; we have room with Raymond's sister..." She gestured her arm towards the door behind the kitchen. "Always." She looked at me dramatically, her face full with empathy.

I heard Raymond scoff from behind me. "You're putting her with Jeanette?" He rolled his eyes. "I would rather room with Grandmother!"

Mrs. Collins sucked in her lips, thumping her fists against the sink basin. "Do not disrespect your grandmother, Raymond." He threw his head back as if he didn't care. I stayed silent, observing how this family interacted.

"Sorry about him, dear," She said as she wiped the sink water off her hands. "You can stay here with my daughter, Jeanette."

I cleared my throat, "I don't want to disrupt y'all's family."

"Don't worry about that, dear. We're a big family; one more will not make a difference."

My voice wavered as I responded. "Thank you so much, you don't know how much I appreciate this."

"You're very welcome."

Raymond walked up to his mother by the sink, one of his hands in his pockets. "Della is asking her mom if they might come over for tea tonight after she is done with work."

"Tonight?" She looked around the room, "I'll have to clean up. Are you sure that she will help you?"

"If someone convinces her–" He made eye contact with her.

As she poured fruit from a bowl into the sink, she whispered to him, "As long as this helps Estelle and her mother."

He grabbed both of her shoulders. "Thank you." He made his way back over to me. "So what do you want to do before Della comes back?" He studied my bag, still sitting on the kitchen table. "Where'd you get it?" He asked.

"I don't remember." I told him. "I've just always used it for traveling,"

He smirked, "It looks… well loved."

The bag sat sadly on the table. It's broken strap hung by a thread, and the awkward shaped items inside made indentations in the fabric. At a glance, it looked quite unwieldly.

"Do you still have to work at the market the rest of the day?" I asked.

He nodded, "I do, until seven."

I gasped, smiling at him while jumping up and down with an idea.

"What?" He chuckled.

I giggled. "What if I come to work with you?"

He laughed. "Are you sure?"

"Yes, it'll get my mind of my mother. Please?" I urged him.

"She can go!" Mrs. Collins called from the sink.

I grinned, "I can go!" I ran to grab a handful of Krispies, and double-checked everything in my bag.

"You can just leave that here." Raymond told me. He went to open the front door and I followed him out and down the street.

We arrived at the bustling market, and people were everywhere. Raymond lifted wooden crates onto a table behind the cashier stand, piling apples on top of each other in the bin.

"Can you grab the strawberries and put them next to these?" He asked me. The box of strawberries was small, but heavy. They glistened in the sun light.

"Sure." I answered.

He smiled at me. "So how is South Carolina different than here?"

"It's very different." I laughed, hauling another crate on top of the strawberries. "Less people, quieter, different accents."

"Different accents?" He asked. "Like what?"

"Well here," I laughed, "Y'all don't say y'all."

"Y'aaallllll." He tried to imitate a southern drawl. "I did it just now," he chuckled.

Towards the end of Raymond's shift, the sun started to set, casting an orange glow across the marketplace. He unloaded the last of the fruit, and I began to cool down from sweating so much. We walked back down the same street to his house, where we would wait for Della and her mother.

At Raymond's house, the lights were on and it looked lively from the outside. When we arrived inside, Mrs. Collins had cleaned the room and the smell of hot tea filled the air. The tabled was set with glasses, and all the groceries put away. Mrs. Collins had changed into a nice navy blue dress, and had redone her hair.

"Welcome back." She welcomed me in, Raymond following behind. "Della and Nurse Davis should be here any minute."

Raymond sat down at the kitchen table, the same one that had the spilled Krispies on it five hours earlier. I sat down in the seat next to him, tapping my fingers on the tabletop while waiting.

"What is Della's mother like?" I asked Raymond.

Raymond fiddled with his shirtsleeve, and looked up from it to answer. "She's quiet, a little bit curt." He stated. The dining table was made of dark wood, and now positioned at the front of the house by the door.

A feeling of nervousness grew in my stomach. I rocked a bit back and forth in my chair. It began to get dark outside, and I realized I was spending another night alone without my parents, but I tried not to let it show on the outside.

Raymond placed his hand over mine to keep my fingers from tapping on the table.

"Don't worry," he reassured me. "Her mom isn't that scary."

I gave him a nervous smile while I watched his mother wrap herself in a coat and walk out of the front door. He lifted his hand off mine. "She's staying here while we talk to Nurse Davis, right?" I asked, shocked that she just left.

Raymond seemed surprised by my question, as he jerked his head back a bit. "Yeah, of course–" He answered, not taking any notice to his mother leaving the house. I leaned forward in my seat to see Mrs. Collins light a cigarette between the front window curtains.

"Your mother smokes cigarettes?" I asked him through my teeth, sloping in my seat toward him, looking around the room.

"Oh, she does." He shrugged his shoulders, turned back to fiddling with his sleeves. I noticed one of them had a rip in the hem.

"Well, there's another difference of my home for you." I commented.

He raised his eyebrows, "Aye, really?"

"Yes, Raymond. And I have never heard anyone say, 'Aye.'"

He laughed at that.

The front door swung open again, and I heard Mrs. Collins and Della speaking in the middle of a conversation.

"Welcome in Miss Della, Nurse Davis." Mrs. Collins announced.

I stood up from my chair, and walked over to Della and her mother. Nurse Davis had short black coils in her hair, and tan skin covered in freckles. She wore a red coat, and a pair of glasses stuck out of her chest pocket.

Mrs. Collins pulled out two chairs from the table, and motioned for them to sit down. Nurse Davis hung her coat over the back of the chair, and sat down next to an empty chair. Mrs. Collins went to the kitchen to fetch the tea, while Raymond's sister, Jeanette, came out of her room behind the kitchen. She walked quietly down into a seat next to her brother. Della walked around the table and took a spot next to me, shrugging off her coat while saying, "Hi again." She beamed at me.

"Hi." I told her.

Mrs. Collins came back with a nice blue pitcher, steam rolling out of the top when she tilted it to pour the first glass of tea. "Everyone would like some?"

I nodded my head at her.

She went around the circular table, pouring a cup of tea for everybody. She took a seat in the empty chair between Nurse Davis and Jeanette. Jeanette sat with her head down, her eyes staring blankly towards the center of the table.

Raymond noticed me looking at her. "She's quiet." He whispered.

Mrs. Collins started the conversation. "I assume we all know why we're here, correct?" The whole table nodded, Jeanette barely blinking.

Della spoke up, "Estelle," she motioned towards me. "This is my mother, Nurse Davis." Nurse Davis looked at me up and down, as if she was deciding if she approved.

"Nice to meet you, Nurse Davis." I introduced myself. "My name is Estelle Banks."

She nodded at me, with no verbal response, and then looked back toward her daughter. Della pushed her hair out of her face, and then rubbed the back of her neck. "Mom, I'm sure Estelle would love to talk to you."

"Thank you." I whispered to her.

She responded, "Always."

I sat up straight and focused on Nurse Davis. "I just arrived here in Boston yesterday from South Carolina." I told her, not sure where to start. "My mother had recently received letters from my aunt about medical treatments for her, and my aunt offered for Mother to come up here and stay with her. We weren't happy about it, but I hoped it would make her feel better. Oh, we, I mean my father, baby brother, and I. Well, my baby brother doesn't know what's going on, I mean, he is a baby." I laughed nervously, my speech becoming faster. The whole group of people sat silent, expecting me to continue my story. "My mother just recently gave birth to my brother, and she was so excited. We all were." I looked to Mrs. Collins for reassurance. "But after she gave birth, she got sad; very, very sad. She lay in bed for days, and refused to talk or take care of her baby. My aunt Rose mailed her letters, and some of them offered doctors in Boston that could help her. So, Mother traveled up here, but after a few weeks Father and I stopped hearing from her. One night, two days ago, I snuck onto a train in the middle of the night, and came all the way up here."

Nurse Davis was paying great attention, but didn't look very concerned. "Dear child," she spoke to me. "Is your mother not with your aunt?"

I shook my head, but Della had an announcement. "Yes, mother. She checked. And her aunt, who was there, wouldn't let her in."

"Yes," I tried to add into the conversation, but Della continued.

"So this morning, Estelle went back to the market where she met Raymond and then this dull-head followed her, where he tried to beat Raymond up at the market."

"Della!" Raymond whisper yelled, getting angry with Della as I sat in between them.

Now Mrs. Collins looked shocked, turning towards Raymond across the table. "Is this true, Raymond?" Her eyes were wide.

"No, no, no, Ma." He tried to convince her. "He just didn't know who we were, he just tapped me on the shoulder." He reached over and lightly punched Jeanette on the back.

His mother's forehead wrinkled. "We will discuss this later, Raymond."

"He said that if they went to the aunt's house again, that Estelle would be arrested."

Mrs. Collins expression kept growing, "Arrested!" She bounced the palms of her hands on the table. "Raymond, we will have a talk about this."

He still sat slouched in his seat, looking at the ground. From their body positions and expressions, you could tell they were definitely siblings.

Nurse Davis finally made a move to speak. "You said she was recently pregnant?" She asked me. She looked at me with her head tilted down at me, and glanced at me through her eyebrows. She reach into the same pocket with her glasses and took out a notebook and a pencil. She scribbled down an address and ripped the paper out, then reached across the table to hand it to me. Both Raymond on my left and Della on my right leaned over to read the address. "Where is this?" Raymond asked.

She didn't answer him, but continued speaking to me. "If your mother had a nervous breakdown after birth, she would be in a psychiatric hospital, not a general one like mine."

My stomach dropped. "A nervous breakdown? What is that?" I asked.

"I'm not specialized in it." She declared. "But it's a problem going on in her brain." This hospital takes visitors, as long as one of them is a blood relative. So you're in luck here." She took another moment to look me over, "you came here all by yourself?" She looked at her own daughter, right next to me.

Nurse Davis shook her head and clicked her tongue. "I wouldn't know what to do with myself if you ran away, Della."

I felt a choking feeling in my throat, the memory of my Dad alone and mom missing, not knowing where either of us are, closing in on my mind. "Nurse Davis?"

"Mhmm?

"Why would my mother be having nervous breakdowns?" I asked.

She took a deep breath, and paused before she answered my question. "Sometimes after a mother gives birth, it makes their body and mind feel differently than they did before. It may have made your mom's mind feel sad, and her body, feel very tired."

I nodded at her in understanding, even though I wasn't sure why mother would feel sad about Jerry.

"Well, we need to go as soon as possible." Raymond told the group.

Della fidgeted with her hair again. "I agree, tomorrow?" She looked at Raymond's mother, and the two adult women looked between each other. Jeanette suddenly stood up and made her way out of the room.

"Goodnight, honey!" Mrs. Collins called. Jeanette smiled back at her, and mumbled coyly, "love you, Ma."

"Della, you can go if you're supervised. I have work tomorrow." Nurse Davis said.

"It could be a step closer to finding your mother," Mrs. Collins told me from across the table. "I suggest you go."

Raymond gazed between everyone seated. "So we'll go tomorrow?"

"We'll all go tomorrow." Della confirmed. She and her mother stood up from the table, draping their coats over their arms. Raymond and I walked her a few steps to the door while the two moms continued conversing.

"Should we meet for breakfast in the morning?" I asked them.

Della eagerly nodded, "that would be lovely." She leaned forward and wrapped her arms around me, swaying me back and forth. "It was nice to meet you, Estelle. We're going to figure this all out." She reassured me.

Nurse Davis stood behind Della and me, and was waiting for her daughter to let go of me. "Ready to go?" She asked Della. She jumped out of the hug, and waved to Raymond and Mrs. Collins.

"Thank you for the tea." Nurse Davis said.

Raymond, Mrs. Collins, and I stood in the doorway as they walked down the street, the air chilly, but not too cold.

Back inside the house, Mrs. Collins had set up a makeshift cot on Jeanette's bedroom floor. I stood in the back of the kitchen with Raymond and his mother as she punched and fluffed two bed pillows.

"I'm sorry darling." She apologized to me. "We'll find a better situation than this," she pointed to the pile of blankets and pillows on the ground, "tomorrow."

I sighed, extremely appreciative of everything she and Raymond had done for me that day. "No, thank you so much. I am just happy to be sleeping inside tonight."

She pouted her face and dropped the pillow, then walked over to me. She embraced me in a hug, "we're going to make this better for you, Estelle. And we don't mind it a bit."

I smiled inside the hug, my eyes beginning to feel heavy.

"I have to make a deal with you though, dear." She pulled me away from the hug. "Tomorrow, at the hospital," she took a deep breath, "call your father. If Raymond snuck off on a train in the middle of the night, I wouldn't know what I would do. Just let your father know you are all right. Please?"

"I will." I told her, rubbing my eyes with the back of my hands. "I promise."

Her hands were still on my shoulders, and she patted them once before stepping away. "Thank you." She walked over to Raymond, who had been observing from the sink. Mrs. Collins leaned over to give him a kiss on the forehead. "Goodnight, love."

He yawned, "Goodnight Ma."

I made my way into the bedroom, the lights all turned off as Jeanette was sound asleep in her bed. Mrs. Collins had placed my bag next to the blanket cot. Raymond stood in the doorway, silent.

"Thank you so, so much." I told him. "I hope your family knows how much I appreciate y'all letting me into your home."

He stared between his feet and the ceiling. "It's really no problem." He finally decided to look at me, and slightly smiled.

"Goodnight, Raymond. See you in the morning."

"Night, Estelle." He turned around and closed the door on me, leaving me in the dark room with his sleeping sister.

I lowered myself onto the cot, the layers of blankets providing a cushion from the wooden floor. I had two pillows lying flat against my head. I twisted and turned in the silence, my body tired but my mind wide awake. I felt for my bag next to me in the dark, and scooped the blue clay bird out of it. I held it to my chest, and lied back down on my side. I wondered what my father was doing, how he was sleeping without knowing if Mother and me where okay and well. I felt guilty leaving him all alone with Jerry, how was he able to work and care for him at the same time? I reassured myself that I would call him in the morning, and that I owed him a huge explanation. How was I going to call him if we didn't own a telephone?

I hugged the bird closer to my chest. This bird, broken and all, was the only thing I had with me that also knew my family, my house, and my mother. I gave it a kiss on the beak, and slowly drifted off to sleep. The only thought that stayed in the back of my mind was, where was Mr. King now, and why did he and my aunt want me gone, and what did they do with my mother.

8

Loud banging erupted from behind the bedroom door. I sat up in the makeshift bed, and felt a crick in my neck.

"Estelle!" Raymond yelled from the other side of the door. "Are you awake? We have to leave!"

The sun was peeking through the curtains, and Raymond's sister, Jeanette, wasn't in her bed. "One moment!" I yelled back at him. I rubbed my eyes, and tried to pat down my tangled hair.

I heard him sigh through the door as I stood up and shook off the sleepiness. "Della's waiting! We're going to meet with her, remember?"

I pulled my shoes on while standing up as fast I could, tripping over myself. The blankets lay crumpled up on the floor, the pillows flat and sideways. I grabbed my bag, and pulled out the clothes I'd brought. I took off my dress, and replaced it with my light blue sweater and navy midi skirt. "Let me get ready, Raymond." I called. "Have patience!" I knelt down and tried to fold the sheets and blankets as nicely as I could for Mrs. Collins. I met Raymond outside of the room carrying the notecard with the address that Nurse Davis had written down for me.

"Ready now?" He complained. He threw his head back, his hair wet.

I nodded, still fully trying to wake up.

He scoffed, "Finally."

I laughed, and he bumped my shoulder with his and said, "We'll meet Della outside," as we walked through the kitchen.

We went down the red brick stairs on his front porch, the thin black metal railing cold when I touched it. The sky was grey and cloudy today, even in the summer. Wind picked up my already tangled hair, and blew it around vigorously. Della was standing on the sidewalk at the end of the stairs. She wore a red dress and beige coat, and had her hair put up with pins.

"Good morning!" She called cheerfully. "Want to go to the cafe?"

We made our way down the street, and followed the same path we would take to the market. Passing the market, we stopped at a small restaurant that smelled like toast and coffee. Inside the restaurant, we sat down at a small table by the window. With my back against the window, I faced Della and Raymond and laid the paper with the address out in front of them.

"Do y'all know where this is?"

Raymond whistled and Della's eyes grew wide when they read the note. They looked at each other, then Raymond look back at me.

He sighed. "That's a while away, Estelle."

I felt my stomach drop. "How far away? Is it too far?" I started to panic.

"We could walk; it would just take a long time." Della reassured me. I tried to think about the whole reason I came to Boston, and how the opportunity to find her arose.

Raymond perked up, slapping his hands on the table. "What if we leave right now?"

"This minute?" Della was shocked. "We just got here!"

Raymond grabbed the note, pushing his chair back with a screech as he stood up. "Forty five minutes if we leave right now." He smiled, and then looked out of the window behind me.

Della grabbed her coat off the back of her chair. "You're feeling energetic." She commented.

"He's been like this all morning." I replied.

Raymond rushed to the front of the cafe, then made his way out, leaving Della and I behind. We ran to catch up with him, causing a noisy scene in the restaurant. We turned the corner out of the door, and saw him jogging down the sidewalk. We ran through the crowds of people, stopping to stand on our tiptoes to try to spot him while laughing. We caught up to him at an intersection, where he was grinning and excited.

The group of people in front of us crossed the street, and we chased after Raymond as he began to push his way through the crowd.

"Run!" He turned back to yell at us.

After a long, tiring, journey to the hospital, we landed in front of a large brick institution. It had many, many, windows, and arches in front of the main entrance. The garden surrounding it looked perfectly manicured, the bushes trimmed and the grass mowed.

Della sat down on the stairs, her hand on her chest, catching her breath. Raymond stared at the building in awe, his hands on his hips as he winded down. I walked past them and up the staircase, my mood changing knowing my mother could be inside.

Inside the hospital, we walked into a large, clean lobby. A wooden desk was positioned in the center of the room, where a nurse was seated, writing something down. The three of us went up the desk without making a sound. Della and Raymond stopped behind me. I looked back at them, and noticed Raymond's mood had changed. His face was stern and he was quiet, he gestured towards the desk with his hand, and whispered, "You should do it."

The nurse at the desk wore large red glasses, and sat scribbling down notes furiously. "Excuse me, Ma'am." I squeaked out. The woman didn't notice me. I glanced behind me to see Della grimace, and Raymond was shaking his head. "What do I do?" I whisper yelled, hoping the nurse wouldn't hear.

"Just get her attention!" Raymond murmured aggressively through his teeth.

I turned back to the nurse and set my hands on the desk. "Good morning." I said louder, leaning slightly over the desk.

The nurse jumped, her focus turning to me. She plastered on a smile and responded to me. "Good morning! How may I help you?"

"I'm here to see my mother." I told her.

She made a small frown at me. "Aw." She pulled a book out of the desk drawer, and opened it to a list of names.

"Your mother's name, please?" She asked.

I took a deep breath to control myself. "Mary Banks."

The nurse swiped through the pages, muttering, "Banks, Banks, Banks..." She looked up at me, "Sorry, Hon. No Banks here."

I felt my face grow hot and my eyes water. "No, no Ma'am," I urged her, looking over the desk farther at the book. "She'll be here." I assured her.

She checked over the names again, and then shook her head. "I'm sorry." She closed the book and picked up the pen again, dismissing me.

I felt Della's hand on my shoulder. "What's her maiden name?" She asked.

My body froze. Her maiden name. "Ward." I mumbled. My breathing stopped, I couldn't speak.

"Excuse me, Hon?" The nurse probed with her Boston accent. "Didn't hear ya."

"Ward. Mary Ward." I gasped out.

The nurse clicked her tongue. "Hear you are." She used her pen to point to the name. *Mary E. Ward.* She pulled the book away as soon as I looked. "Relation to the patient?"

"Daughter, ma'am." I could barely speak, my body felt heavy.

The nurse groaned. "Sorry, you might have the wrong patient. Mary E. Ward has only one living relative. According to my sheet, she was discharged last week to a living sibling."

My heart was racing, and my legs began to feel wobbly.

"Estelle?" I heard Raymond behind me. "Are you feeling well?" His voice was in front of me now.

"Everything will be fine, you're okay." I heard Della now, and felt her grab onto my arm.

"Why did she use her maiden name?" I asked, waiting for anyone to answer. Raymond knelt down in front of me. "Her only living relative?" I couldn't get the words out of my mouth. "I'm her daughter." My head spun and I couldn't feel any part of my body.

"Estelle, sit down. Try to be calm." Della lowered me to the ground, my knees touching the cold marble. Tears streamed down my face, and I squinted my eyes to get them to stop.

Raymond was in front of me, looking directly at me. "I'm her daughter!" I shrieked. I sobbed, leaning forward towards the floor. Raymond caught me, his arms around me. Della leaned over, hugging me from behind and patting my hair.

"Shhh..." She said. "We'll figure this out." Raymond and Della exchanged worried glances, and Raymond shifted my body weight onto Della. I was leaning back in her lap, and she rocked me back and forth. Raymond stood up and walked back over to the desk.

After a moment of silence between Della and me, she asked, "Do you still want to call your father?"

I nodded my head. "Yes. I just need a moment." I sniffled.

Della helped me up, and led me to a telephone. It sat on a side table next to the waiting room sofa.

"We don't own a telephone." I told her. "How am I going to reach him?"

Della stood there, looking around the room as she thought. "Do you have a neighbor, or family friend that could deliver a message?" She wondered.

"I do."

Della smiled, and then walked towards Raymond to give me some privacy. I sat on the sofa and reached over to the telephone, dialing the only number I knew by heart. The phone buzzed, until I heard a familiar male voice on the other end.

"This is Mr. Saunders, how may I help you?" The voice said.

I exhaled. "Mr. Saunders, is Vivian home?"

I heard a crash on the other end of the call. "Estelle!" Mr. Saunders hollered. "Dear Lord! We have been worried sick! Your father..." He stopped. "He has been a mess."

I felt guilty. "I am so sorry, sir. I do really need to speak with Vivian."

I heard Mr. Saunders yell, "Vivian!" Then silence filled the call.

"Estelle?' Shrieked Vivian. "Is it really you?"

I laughed, wiping my cheeks dry. "Yes, it's me."

"Oh, Estelle! I can't believe it; everyone has been so scared for you!"

"Listen, ViVi. I cannot talk very much right now. I need you to speak to my father for me."

Her voice dropped. "Oh, sure."

I took a deep breath. "Tell him that I am so sorry, but that I went to Boston to find Mother. Tell him that I have a plan so that he doesn't worry, and that when he sees me next, I'll be with Mother. Can you have him come to the phone later, so I can talk to him?"

"Yes." She let out. "When?"

"Tonight, maybe? I'll try to find another telephone. Again, tell him I am so, so, sorry."

I heard Vivian gulp. "I'll do that."

"Thank you so much. I have to leave, but it sounds nice hearing your voice," I told her.

She made a noise as if she was crying, "Yours, too. I miss you Estelle."

I sighed. "I miss you too, ViVi. Goodbye."

"Goodbye."

I set the telephone back down, and saw Della and Raymond back at the desk, arguing with the nurse. I caught Della's eyes, and she rushed over to me when she saw I was done with the telephone.

"How did it go?" She asked, grabbing my hands.

My voice was shaky, "He'll be by the phone tonight."

"Oh, that's good." She wiped a tear from my cheek with her finger. "The nurse at the desk told us that Mary had been checked out permanently, but wouldn't say more."

I sniffled. "Why wouldn't she use her real name?" I looked at her.

Raymond walked up behind her, interrupting.

Della helped me up. "Did you find anything else?" She asked.

He nodded. "I walked around a bit and heard two doctors arguing in the hallway."

"Doctors?" I asked.

"Yeah." I he looked around. He began to whisper, "They said something like 'she knows Mary was here.'"

Della's jaw dropped.

"What?" I shrieked.

Raymond continued, "They were arguing about if they should tell the caregiver to relocate her or not."

"What does that mean? Caregiver!" I walked back from them. "Did Rose take her? Did she take my mother?" I breathed heavily.

Della's tone grew serious. "Did they see you?"

"Who?" Raymond's brows furrowed.

"The doctors!" Della and I yelled in unison. The nurse at the desk gave us a look.

Raymond shook his head, looking at the ground. "No, I don't think so."

I held my hands to my head, spinning around. "Oh, my god. We need to find her before she hides her. Could we call the police?" I looked between them helplessly.

Della's eyes grew wide. "No, absolutely not." She was curt. "If your aunt is as wealthy as we think she is, she'll have connections."

"She's right." Raymond added.

I walked past them, through the main lobby of the hospital. A bald man in a white shirt stared as I walked past him, and I put my head down.

Footsteps snuck up behind me. "That was one of them," Raymond whispered. I looked back, and made eye contact with the doctor. His eyes followed me as we walked through the door.

9

The walk back to Raymond's house was a long one. It was almost noon, but the streets had calmed down since this morning. Della and Raymond stood on either side of me. It was cloudy and humid, my hair sticking to the back of my neck. The air was damp and dew was forming on lampposts as we walked by them. We went past buildings with many winding staircases, and advertisements posted on the walls. Turning the corner of the street, we walked beside an incredibly charming park lined with green trees and decorative metal fencing.

"I need to call my father later." I told them quietly.

Della smiled at me, and grabbed my hand. "We'll be there with you."

"We will." Raymond assured me as well. He grabbed my other hand as the three of us continued walking.

Della squeezed my hand and let go. "I know where we could go to find a telephone." She bounced from foot to foot. Raymond hadn't let go.

He looked at her questioningly. "Where, Della." He was smiling.

She ran out in front of us and did a little spin yelling, "The Swing Club!" She giggled. Her tone was very bubbly.

Raymond rolled his eyes, and finally let go of my hand. "How do you figure we could get into the Swing Club?"

"We don't have to actually eat there." She was still grinning wide as we continued walking. "We just have to get in, let Estelle use the phone, and leave!" She bumped my shoulder and smirked at me. "And maybe have a little fun, too!"

Raymond scoffed at her. "Get in?" He raised his eyebrows. "You mean we'll probably have to sneak in." He sighed. "They have that fancy dress code and the entry fee..." he trailed off.

I stopped in my tracks, my chest feeling light, "Entry fee?" I smiled at Raymond. "I can help with that!"

Della giggled next to me, "Let's go!" She grabbed my arm.

Raymond put his hand on my shoulder, slowing us down. "I have to be at the market until seven tonight." He stared at us.

Della shrugged her shoulders. "We can go after."

"What will we all wear?" He asked.

Della looked up and down at both Raymond and I. "Estelle can wear something of mine, and Raymond," she jutted her lip out, "maybe you can wear something of my dad's."

"Fine, but the main reason we're there is for the telephone, remember?"

"Oh, of course!" Della and I laughed as we continued walking, letting Raymond trail behind us.

We arrived at Raymond's house weary, and Raymond was not excited to go to work.

"I've got to go quickly," he told us, rushing around the room drinking a glass of water. "I have already missed my shift this morning." He finished chugging the drink. "Do you two want to come help?"

I began to nod when I noticed Della next to me. "Estelle and I can have some girl time," she informed him. "We can find outfits for tonight."

Raymond frowned at me.

"Sure," I nodded, agreeing with Della. "We will do that."

Raymond left the house, and headed for the market.

Della sat in the one of the kitchen seats. "You ever been to a swing club?" She asked, admiring her fingernails. "I assume you haven't." She looked up at me.

"No, I haven't." I answered. "What are they like?"

She fixed her posture in the chair, her eyes lighting up. "Well," she started, "they are so glamorous and luxurious. Men in suits take your take your orders for your meal, and a singer or band is always performing on the stage. The lights are dim, and people are always laughing." She started to look off into the room. "People can get up and dance whenever they like, it's just magical." She sighed.

"Really? How often do you go?" I asked.

She frowned. "I've only been once, for my uncle's wedding. We can't normally afford to go."

I took a deep breath. "Well, we can have fun tonight!" I tried to reassure her. "What should we wear?"

She stood up from the chair, rubbing her hands together. "Let's look through my clothes!" She was smiling widely now.

We walked to Della's home, right next to Raymond's house. Her entryway was small, the kitchen inside smaller. A single lamp stood by the kitchen table, but she didn't turn any of the lights on.

"Follow me upstairs!" She ran up the staircase, the wooden planks creaking from old age beneath her feet. A narrow hallway appeared at the top of the stairs, with two doors on either side. Pale green carpet lined the floors, and there was no furniture. On the other hand, Della's room was full of collected items and knick-knacks, including a pair of tall brown boots, which sat by the doorframe.

"You can take a seat." She pointed me towards an armchair by her bedroom window. She knelt down to open up her dresser drawer, pulling out a stack of folded dresses. She set the stack down and held the first one out in front of me.

"Do you like this one?" She asked. "I think the blue could be pretty on you, match your eyes."

I nodded and smiled, then pointed to a brown dress in the pile. "What about that one for you?" I suggested.

"To match my eyes!" She exclaimed. "How about we look for something for Ray?" She proposed. I nodded.

We snuck into her parent's bedroom, and she grabbed a nice shirt and jacket that were hanging on a wooden hanger.

"Do you think these could work for him?" She was trying not to laugh.

"Let's have him wear it." I demanded, my giggles causing Della to burst out laughing.

Della and I changed into our dresses, and looked at ourselves in her mirror. Her mirror hung on the wall above her dresser, which was covered with jars and boxes of random items. Della picked up a metal tin and opened it, revealing a tiny golden tube. She twisted the cap off, and applied bright red lipstick.

She noticed me looking at it, and held it out in front of me. "Want to use it?" She offered.

"Sure." I grabbed it from her, trying it on my lips.

She opened another metal tin, this one square with pink powder inside. She dipped her finger in a glass of water, then in the powder, and then applied it to her cheeks in the mirror.

I looked at myself in the mirror, noticing the change in my appearance. My hair was oily and my eyes had dark circles underneath them. My lips were chapped, and Della's red lipstick felt crusty.

"Ready to go?" Della had walked over and folded up the clothes for Raymond.

I smiled, "Yes."

Della and I sat in Raymond's kitchen until he got home from work. He opened the door, and I stood up to hand him his new clothes.

"What is this?" He seemed nervous, fingering through the shirts.

I laughed at him. "It's for you to wear tonight." I went to stand behind him, and nudged him towards the bathroom. "Try them on, go on."

Raymond threw his head back, regretting what he was doing. He walked into the bathroom, and Della and I stood outside waiting.

The bathroom door opened with a force. He strutted out, wearing Della's father's suit. "I look ridiculous!" He stuck his arms out and spun around, giving us a fashion show.

"Estelle, do you have the money?" Della turned around towards me.

I pointed towards the bedroom door. "I'll go get it."

Once in the bedroom, I rummaged through my bag, and fished out the envelope from the bottom. I brought it out to Raymond, and he stuck it in his pocket.

"Be careful with that." I cautioned him. We walked out of his house, and headed for the club.

It was dark outside by the time we arrived. The restaurant was only a mile away from Raymond's, but the area of town was completely different. We stood on the sidewalk facing the building, waiting for our chance in line. A tall woman walked past us, wearing floor length silky gown and a fur coat. She passed the entire line, and the guards let her in without a word. *ViVi would love to see a star like her,* I thought to myself.

We approached the top of the line, Della and I standing behind Raymond.

"Do you have club access?" A security man in a suit asked Raymond. He was taller than Raymond was and he wore a blunt expression.

Raymond shook his head. "No, sir."

"Would you like to pay the fee, then?" He urged.

"We would." Raymond responded. He reached into his jacket pocket, pulling out my envelope of money. The paper had worn down from its long journey, but the money was still there.

The man looked Raymond up and down. "How many are joining us tonight?"

Raymond turned back to look at us. "Only three."

"Is there an adult in this group?" The man glanced behind Raymond at Della and me.

"Yes, sir, I am."

Della giggled in my ear to Raymond's lie as Raymond gave the man our money.

He pocketed the money, and opened the doors for our group. "Have a pleasant night."

I followed Raymond and Della inside, and acknowledged the security guard. "Thank you, sir."

The inside of the restaurant was magical. We walked in, the faint sound of music coming from further inside the building. There was a sitting room by the entryway, where a group of people in luxurious clothes sat and drank. We continued further into the building, and the music grew louder. Tables were full of people chatting, laughing, and having fun. Waiters brought out large platters of food, presenting them to the customers.

I saw Della staring at one of the dishes, and I reminded her, "We're here for the telephone. Only."

She smiled back at me. "You're right."

As we continued into the club, we came upon a large hallway, filled to the brim with people dancing. A group of musicians stood near the back of the hall, singing and playing the trumpet. I looked all around me, at the tall ceiling with detailed crowning, and at the wooden floor where women's heels had left imprints from dancing. I looked at Raymond and Della, and wanted to express my exceptional gratitude to them for helping me. I glanced around in awe, but kept peeking at Raymond.

Della began to clap her hands in tune with the music and then she grabbed my arms and spun me around. "Dance, Estelle!"

I threw my head back and laughed with her, swaying along to the music.

We danced until the song ended and another one began. The room was very crowded and lively. The song picked up in tempo, and everyone was cheering for each other. Della let go of both of my hands and traded me off to Raymond.

I almost tripped into him, but he helped me to catch my balance. "I like this music!" I told him, raising my voice so he could hear me over the noise.

"Me too!" He shouted back at me. "Want to dance?" He asked.

I chuckled. "Sure."

He grabbed my hand and spun me around, then held me still again.

"Thank you for helping me." I told him. "And Della, too."

"Of course."

We swayed in the dance hall for a few more minutes, the music calming me. An unfamiliar feeling arose in my stomach. *Is this what Mother and Father felt?* I asked myself. I thought back to when Mother was pregnant, and how her and Father stood in the entryway to our kitchen.

"Don't be impolite!" Mother had yelled at me. *"You'll love somebody someday as well."*

I wish I hadn't groaned at the idea of Mother and Father showing affection, and I thought about how much I wish I could see them share that moment right now. But, Aunt Rose had abducted Mother and Father was at home, 1,000 miles away from her. *Is this feeling that I have the one Mother had told me about?* I asked myself.

I smiled up at Raymond. "Ever been dancing?" He wondered.

"Nope." I giggled.

I turned away from him, and felt someone's eyes on me. Behind my shoulder, a short, stubby man with a moustache had noticed me from across the room. I ignored him, but a grim feeling stuck around in my stomach.

Raymond noticed my discomposure. "Is everything okay?" He puzzled.

"Yeah," I reassured him. "I'm fine." He kept swaying me, but I checked across the room every few seconds.

Raymond abruptly stopped. "What's happening?" He really wanted to know.

The man in the flimsy hat was still there, across the room. He stood very still, staring directly at me. Only me.

I gasped. "Raymond!" I whisper-yelled, tapping him repeatedly on the front of the shoulder.

"What?" He stammered.

I cleared my throat, "That man," I whispered.

He looked confused, "Who?"

"Let's spin." I told him. We spun to face the other direction. I couldn't see the man now, but described him to Raymond while facing the opposite direction. "He's wearing a suit and hat, staring at me– in the corner over there."

Raymond was silent, trying to spot the man. I turned us a little bit. "In the far back, behind the dining tables," I showed him.

"Oh my god." He let out. "Is that…"

"I think so." I said quietly, blinking rapidly.

I quickly turned towards him, standing in front of Raymond. He continued to stare, then smirked and tipped his hat towards me.

I heard Raymond behind me, mumbling. I stood still, facing the same direction. "What's he doing here?" Raymond rubbed his forehead, frantically looking around the room.

"Get Della." I demanded, staying as frozen as a rock.

Raymond didn't move from his crazed pacing.

"Ray, get Della!" I yelled. He turned around, pushing through dancers to find her. Mr. King, the man leering, had ducked down out of my eyesight and left.

Della and Raymond came rushing towards me, Della's face full of concern. "What is happening?" She asked me, gripping my wrists.

"King's here." Raymond answered, surveying the room for him.

Della gawked, her eyes wide, staring between Raymond and me in disbelief. "Estelle, we need to get you to a telephone."

"You're right." I said.

Della led the way, holding onto one of my hands while running through the club in front of me. We weaved in between dancers, and ducked underneath waiters carrying plates over our heads.

"Estelle, why is he here?" Della called back to me, still sprinting.

I clenched my fists. "He was following me, I bet!" I hollered back at her.

"He wants your location?" Her voice was squeaky.

"Aunt Rose must've sent him; he had to have followed us here!"

We ran into the lounge where the other guests had been sitting and enjoying themselves earlier. The green velvet sofas were empty, and empty glasses had been left on the short dark wooden coffee table. Across from one of the sofas was a tall dark chest, with a telephone displayed on top. I rushed over to it, frantically dialing the Saunders' telephone number.

The line rang, until a deep voice picked up. "Estelle?" It asked.

I mumbled, "It's me."

"This is Mr. Saunders again," he stopped, and took a deep breath. "Your father is in the room with me." I heard him hand the telephone to my father, and then I heard his voice.

"Estelle?" The voice was blunt.

My voice choked, "Father?"

"You are in *Boston*." He stated.

I stayed quiet.

"Estelle, answer me!"

"Yes." I let out quickly. "I am."

There was a period of quietness over the phone, until he addressed me. "I've been very worried. We all are." He was very stern. "I am angry with you; I will be for a while. Stealing money, Estelle?" His voice got higher. "But I want to know that you are safe. And that you are with your mother and," he stopped. "Your aunt."

I bit my lip. "I went to Aunt Rose's house." I told him the truth. "She didn't let me in, and then she sent her little henchman after me, and he threatened to arrest me," I started ranting quickly. "And I made friends that I am staying with, and Mrs. Collins has been so nice," I gasped for a breath, "And we checked the hospital, because Della's mother is a nurse, but they said that Mother had checked in under her maiden name." My foot started bouncing frantically on the ground, and I was gripping the phone as hard as I could. "The front desk lady told me that Mother had said that her only blood relative was Rose, and that she didn't have any children, and that she hadn't been pregnant—"

"Honey!" Father cut me off. "Slow down, Estelle, who are Mrs. Collins, and Della?"

I took in a few deep breathes to slow myself down. "I've been staying at Mrs. Collins' house, she runs the market here.

And Della is her neighbor. She's my age, you would like her." I closed my eyes to concentrate on the story. "But while we were at the hospital, Raymond overheard two doctors saying that Rose had checked mother out, and was taking her some-place other than the home."

"Raymond? Who is that?" He interrogated me.

I groaned. "Mrs. Collins' son, he works at the market." I continued, "Rose had sent this man, her henchman, like I said, called Mr. King. He told me if I ever came near her, I would be in a lot of trouble." I stopped. "Big trouble," I whispered, looking around me. "We're at a restaurant right now, so I could use the telephone, and Mr. King followed us here. I think he has been following me everywhere. I am scared, Father."

"Do you know where your mother is now, Estelle?" He was adamant.

"No, Rose took her away. Do you know where they could've gone, another hospital?" I asked him.

He kept quiet, thinking about my question. "This is a probability." He started, "Your mother's family had a summer cabin, deep in the forest." Quiet again. "If Rose wanted to be hidden, she would've gone there."

A ton of pressure released from my mind. "Oh, thank you, Father." I was extremely grateful.

"Wait," he called through the telephone. "I don't feel that you are safe doing this on your own."

"On my own?"

"I think I should be there with you, Estelle." He proposed.

My eyebrows flew to the top of my forehead. "What?" I spat out.

"You do not get a say in this, Estelle." He informed me. "It might take two days by car, but Jerry and I will be there. Where are you staying?"

I gave him Raymond's address, shocked that he was coming to Boston.

"I love you, Estelle." He told me.

My face flushed. "I love you too, Father."

"I will see you in two days."

"Goodbye." I set the phone down slowly, unfocused. My vision was cloudy, and I faced Della. She was laying down on the green sofa, making herself comfortable. She saw me, and sat up on her elbows.

"What did he say?" She asked.

"He's driving up to Boston." I told her, stunned. My ears almost began to ring.

Her jaw dropped open, and she swiveled herself out of her seat. "Your father? What about your brother?"

"He is coming too; they'll be here in two days."

Della's grin grew wide. "Whoa, two days?" She bounced on her feet. "That is amazing, Estelle!"

I sat down on the sofa limply, where she had been. "He told me that Aunt Rose may have taken her to a cabin."

"A cabin?" She scowled. "Who lives in a cabin?"

I sighed, staring at the floor. "It was her family's summer home. I think she's there so that I won't find her." I began to cry, a tear falling down my cheek.

Della knelt by the sofa. "Aye, it's going to be fine, Estelle. We can find her." She smiled at me.

Raymond turned the corner into the lounge, out of breath from running. "He's gone." He declared. "I can't find him, he left." He panted, leaning down with his hands on his knees. He looked closer at us, and noticed I was crying. "Did you call your father?" He came over to stand behind Della.

I nodded, wiping my tears away. "Rose took my mother to a secret cabin, only my father really knows where it is. He's coming up here in two days."

Raymond raised his eyebrows. "He'll be here," he pointed at the ground, "in two days?"

"Yeah," I almost laughed, "he will."

Raymond blinked rapidly. "So he can just show us where the cabin is, right?" He said, nonchalantly.

Della and I looked at him, realizing he was right.

"So when Mr. Banks arrives, we'll go to the cabin, fight off the evil witch, and save Estelle's mother." He chuckled. "Seems easy enough–"

I stood up, fidgeting with my fingers. "I guess we should go back home, now."

Della nodded, "My father must be wondering where his suit went." She tried to lighten the mood.

Raymond, Della, and I, walked out of the restaurant, and into the busy Boston downtown. I breathed deeply into the night air, looking up into the stars while Raymond and Della chatted. My borrowed, blue dress flowed in the wind, and I crossed my arms in front of me to secure myself. *Maybe Mother can see the same stars from the cabin as I see. I thought to myself. Wherever she is.*

10

I woke up on the floor, my head pounding. Jeanette laid asleep on her bed; this was first time she ever slept in. I sat up on my forearms, yawning. Mrs. Collins had washed the dress I had arrived in, and hung it for me on the back of a desk chair in the room. I put the dress on quickly, hoping Jeanette wouldn't wake up.

The smell of bacon wafted through the air and under the door, filling up the bedroom. I heard a stirring noise come from the kitchen. I cracked open the bedroom door, peaking to the right, into the kitchen. Mrs. Collins was whisking something in a bowl, humming to herself. She spotted me looking through the door, set down the bowl and whisk, and motioned for me, "Oh, come in, come in, Sweetie!"

"Good morning." I told her, trudging into the kitchen. I took a seat at the kitchen table. I watched Mrs. Collins as she plated a few pieces of bacon for me.

"Do you want any eggs?" She offered.

I shook my head as she set the plate in front of me.

She sighed. "Worried about today?" She asked.

"I guess I am." I confided in her. She walked back into the kitchen, pouring a couple glasses of orange juice. "I know he is angry with me."

She tried to reassure me. "If Raymond had ran away, and I was given the opportunity to help and find him, especially if he had run away because of a situation of the caliber of your Mother's," she paused. "I would just be happy to see him again."

I nodded, picking at my food. "Thank you."

She smiled, going back to her cooking.

I heard footsteps coming down the stairs, they were Raymond's; he appeared with disheveled hair, rubbing his eyes. He stopped on the stairs when he noticed me.

"You're up early." He said.

I tried to laugh, my leg bouncing anxiously on the floor.

"She's nervous." Mrs. Collins told him.

He laughed, then came and sat at the table next to me. Mrs. Collins brought him one of the other plates of food.

Raymond shoved a bite of scrambled egg into his mouth. I began to feel excited about my father's arrival, and nervously kept my eye on the front door. After a little more conversation with Mrs. Collins, I heard a familiar sound coming from outside the building.

I jumped from my seat, running to the window. I pressed my hands against it, trying to get a view of the street outside. A man in the car outside waved at me through the windows. It was Father! I jerked open the front door, running outside without closing it behind me. Father parked on the side of the road by Raymond's house. I watched him get out of the car, then lumber to the other door to get Jerry out.

"Father!" I yelled. I was ecstatic to see them, and I rushed down the porch stairs to the car.

"It feels great knowing you are well, Estelle." He told me, grinning. Father left his bags in the car, while he held Jerry. I ran and grabbed Jerry from him, then gave them both a big squeeze.

I looked around behind me to see Mrs. Collins and Raymond waving from the door. Mrs. Collins crossed her arms over her heart and made a pouting face at Jerry.

"Welcome to Boston!" Mrs. Collins called.

Father smiled back at her, being his usual quiet self. He looked at Jerry, then bent forward and spoke quietly. "I need to speak with you about your mother." He informed me.

He had a very serious tone.

I nodded at him, showing him I'd talk with him. Father and I followed Mrs. Collins and Raymond inside their house. Once indoors, Mrs. Collins walked toward Jerry, sticking her hands in front of her with a grabbing motion. I handed him off to her, giving him one last kiss on the forehead. Mrs. Collins went off bouncing him in her arms.

Father sat down at the kitchen table, taking in his surroundings. "You have been here this whole time? With strangers? Honey..." I couldn't tell if he was angry or concerned.

"They invited me, Father." I wanted to convince him. "Mrs. Collins washed my dress, and makes me breakfast." I pointed to the unfinished plate beside me. I change the topic of conversation, "We need to go to the cabin as soon as possible." I urged him.

"Listen, Estelle." He grabbed my hand from across the table.

"What?" I asked him, wondering what could be so serious.

He took in a deep breath. "There are many stories of women that go into psychiatric hospitals, and when they come out," He paused. "They are different, different from before."

I didn't say anything to him.

"They receive therapy for their depression," he said. "It sends shocks through their bodies, inducing comas."

My mouth opened, and it felt like my throat was closing.

"Sometimes, not always, but sometimes," he looked intensely at me, "this can cause their memories to leave them."

"Those are only stories though, right?" I asked him, scared to look at him for what he would say.

He said nothing.

I began to feel very angry, not scared like I had been before. I stood up in front of him, my chair screeching across the floor loudly.

"We need to leave now." I told him. "Raymond!" I called. I ran into the bedroom behind the kitchen, where my bag sat neatly on the desk. I crumpled my old clothes into my bag, and then lugged it over my shoulder, the handles still broken. I charged through the kitchen, as Raymond came downstairs.

"What's happening?" He asked me, his eyes wide.

I continued walking, "we're going to the cabin."

I heard him scoff behind me.

Mrs. Collins appeared back in the room, patting Jerry on his bald head. "Is everything okay?" She was very concerned.

Raymond responded to his mother, "We're going to find Estelle's mother." Now Raymond was rushing to leave, looking frantically around his house.

Father had already gone outside to the car, and I ran through the front door. I leaped over the stairs, almost falling into the automobile. Raymond came next, stomping his feet down the stairs. I yanked open the passenger door, throwing my bag onto the floorboard. Father turned the key to start the engine. I motioned at Raymond to get Della. He ran to get her, banging on her front door. I scooted into the passenger seat, where Mother had always sat.

Della ran out of her door, exchanging words with Raymond. She hopped to put her shoes on, and then followed Ray to the car. They got into the back two seats, slamming the doors behind them.

Father started to drive off in the car, and we watched Mrs. Collins standing on her front porch, looking down at us, holding Jerry in her arms.

During the drive, Father told Della, Raymond, and I about Mother's experience in the cabin during her childhood.

"Estelle, your mother and her family went there every summer." He was driving through the streets as fast as he could, even with all of the cars around us. "She always told me it was one of her happy places."

I watched as we drove underneath those tall buildings that had begun to seem familiar. "Why did we never go visit?" I asked.

"Your Aunt Rose inherited it. It's the only thing she received from your grandparents, and after your mother moved down to South Carolina, Rose never invited her back."

Della spoke up form the back. "Oh, that's so sad." I looked at her; her eyes wore dark circles under them from tiredness.

During the duration of the drive, Della, Raymond, Father, and I were silent. I still felt like Father was angry with me for leaving. *He should be.* I thought to myself.

I thought more about the Doctors at the hospital, and that the nurse at the front desk said that Mother hadn't mentioned anything about a family. I thought it was bizarre for Mother not to have conversations about her kids, but now it began to make sense.

"Father?" I turned to look at him. He was staring straight ahead, focusing on his driving. I continued to speak even without a response from him. "Aunt Rose must have checked Mother into the hospital, purposely leaving out critical information." I turned to sit backwards, looking at Raymond and Della over the headrest. "If Mother received those treatments, and her memory faded," I grimaced at the thought. "That explains why she wouldn't have corrected the details."

I turned back to sit correctly, the pieces of information I had just put together really sinking in. I felt my throat start to close, but instead of becoming distressed, I tried to turn my thoughts into confidence. I took deep breaths, in and out.

"Mr. King followed us multiple times." I told Father. "I don't want him to hurt us, especially if he turns up at the cabin."

"He won't." Raymond said from the back. "If he sees your father, he'll get scared away. Don't worry."

I tried to let that calm me, but it didn't seem entirely true.

The scenery outside changed from the vibrant city of Boston to dirt roads and lush forests as we drove into the middle of nowhere. Raymond offered to help Father with the directions to the cabin.

He said, "My family delivers special shipments to important customers out there sometimes."

After the long, car ride, Father pulled the car through a gravel and dirt driveway.

"I think this is the place." He announced to us. Trees engulfed the driveway and the cabin in front of us. We all got out of the car, standing in the circular drive. Father stood outside of the driver's seat, Della behind him. I stood outside of the passenger seat, Raymond behind me. We were all captivated by the large wooden cabin directly in front of us.

I took a deep breath and started walking forward, everyone following me.

"Is Rose home at the moment?" Raymond asked as we made our way through the driveway. For the first time, he sounded genuinely anxious.

Father shook his head, "the lights are all off." He pointed into all of the windows.

I was the first to arrive at the front door, tugging on its handle. It was locked. I examined the house, hoping there was an open backdoor around the corner.

"Father, Della," I turned around and looked at the two of them. Father was barely taller than Della was. "Y'all should stay in the front, and guard for Aunt Rose, if she decides to come home."

Father objected, "I don't want you going through the woods alone."

"I won't be alone," I nodded at Raymond. "I'll have Raymond."

Della gave my father a shy smile.

"Just be careful." He stuttered. "And let us in quickly."

Raymond and I ventured around the outside of the house. It was eerily quiet, just a few birds chirping in the trees above us.

"Do you believe your Mother is in there?" He asked, moving a tree branch to form a path in front of him.

"I really hope so." I told him. "I can feel it."

Raymond and I had to jump over a fence to get into the property. We walked through a garden in the backyard to reach the door. I pulled on the door, and it opened. We walked inside, and saw that Rose adorned the cabin with extremely nice objects. Photos of Aunt Rose and Mother when they were young lined every surface, and little glass statues sat next to them.

"I thought cabins were supposed to be less fancy." He joked, but he seemed jumpy.

The cabin was dark inside, the only light coming from the windows. A giant staircase was in the middle of the first floor, the banister smooth and polished. The front door was directly across from the staircase, its windows with detailing and patterns. It had three locks from the inside, and I turned each one until I heard a click. I opened it for Father and Della, and they joined Raymond and me inside the cabin.

Della walked in last, and gasped when she looked around at the decorations. "Wow, Estelle." She traced her finger over one of the trinkets on a side table. "How much is this all worth?"

"I cannot believe it." Father sighed.

I walked over to him. "Can't believe what?" I asked.

"Just all of the stories I heard from here." He shrugged.

We all stood around, admiring the first floor of the cabin.

"We need to find her." I told everyone. I led everyone to the staircase. I stepped on the first step and it creaked loudly. I walked up slowly, putting most of my body weight on the banister. The others followed me quietly up the stairs. There was a long hallway, with many, many rooms.

One door at the end of the hallway was the only one cracked open.

"Should we check that one first?" Della whispered.

We all walked through the hallway, a decorative dark red carpet beneath us. I stopped in the doorway after pushing the door open. I was shocked with what I saw when I walked in the room. Mother was in the bed, staring blankly at the wall with no thoughts. She looked skinny, pale, ill, and was shivering. I ran to her, horrified.

"Mother!" I yelled, rushing to hug her in the bed. "What's happened to you?" I cried, feeling her face.

She turned her head at me, "Who?" She whispered as she stared straight forward, almost through me. She was frail, and very confused.

Father came from the doorway, rushed over to help as well. "Mary?" He grabbed her hand, but she looked between us as if she had never seen us before in her life.

I started crying, "What do we do?" I yelled. "What did they do to her?" Raymond hadn't walked into the room yet, and Della stood in the corner with her hands over her mouth.

A loud creaking came from the floor below us. The front door slammed shut, and everyone looked at each other.

"Oh my God." Della squealed, her eyes becoming very wide and her face pale.

Father ran out of the room, and into the hallway to see what was happening.

I reached into my bag, frantically, trying to find something to jog her memory. I grabbed the blue bird, and held it against her hands with mine.

"Oh," She squeaked. She looked at me, actually studying my face.

"Estelle!" Father yelled from outside of the room. He ran in, his eyes wide. Stomping came from up the stairs. Rose appeared in the doorway, fuming with anger.

"You!" She screeched at me. Her dark brown hair was in a bun, her face red. She ran towards me, grabbing for my arm. "What are you doing here?" She bared her teeth, digging her fingernails into my arm.

Father tried to pull her off me, but she screamed and stuck her elbow into his stomach.

"Leave her alone!" He yelled.

Raymond was in the doorway with his hands above his head, watching the commotion.

"Ms. Rose?" A deep voice yelled from the hallway. "What is happening?"

Suddenly, Mr. King burst into the room, glaring at us. He pushed Raymond out of the doorway, knocking him to the ground.

"Stop!" Father yelled, standing over Mother.

Mr. King rumbled over to Rose and me. He pulled her off me, and then grabbed me by my shoulders, holding me in place.

Raymond got up from the floor, his nose bleeding.

"Get out of my house!" Aunt Rose yelled.

Father yelled back at her, "Give me back my wife!"

Mr. King let go of me, then focused his attention on my father.

"Don't disrespect Ms. Rose." He demanded, slapping Father in the face, knocking his glasses off.

Small peeping came from the bed.

"Stop," Mother groaned. "Stop."

Everybody paused, shocked, to stare.

Mother tried to get up from the bed, but couldn't, and fell back into the mattress.

Rose rushed towards her, "You don't know them, Mary." She told her in a baby voice. "They're here to hurt you." Aunt Rose grabbed her hand.

"What?" Mother murmured.

I pushed Aunt Rose out of the way, "Mother, it's Estelle, your daughter." I tried to convince her.

"Oh." She mumbled, gazing at my face.

Father and Raymond were both bleeding. "We need to get her out!" Father ordered.

Della ran downstairs, Raymond following her, holding his nose with his fingers.

Father shoved Aunt Rose to the side, bumping her into the bedside table. He tried to scoop up Mother.

I watched Aunt Rose on the floor, her jaw open. She was defeated.

"Estelle." Mother called, she hadn't taken her eyes off me.

Rose was shocked, "No!" She howled.

Father carried Mother out of the room. I grabbed my bag and the blue bird from the sheets. I followed them, running down the stairs from Mr. King behind me.

Outside, Father helped Mother into the car. Della was sitting in the grass, calming herself down, as Raymond stood by the door of the car with blood all over his face.

Father hollered at everyone, "Get in the car!"

We squeezed into the car, Raymond, Della, and I packed into the back seat. Father started the car, as Aunt Rose came running out of her front door.

"Help!" She screamed, sprinting to the car. "Stop!" She banged her hand onto the window. "Do not leave!"

Father pressed his foot on the accelerator, speeding the car up and away from Aunt Rose.

We arrived back at Raymond's, Father barely stopping the car before he got out. He ran up the stairs, knocking on the door. Raymond and Della followed him, leaving Mother and I alone in the car.

I leaned forward so she could see me from the seat. "I love you." I told her.

She took a long time to respond, blinking at me, trying to find the words. "I love you too." She stuttered.

Father came out of the house carrying Jerry, Mrs. Collins standing behind him. He opened the door, handing Jerry to me.

Della and Raymond stood outside of the car, by my door. I turned the lever to roll down the window, so I could hear both of them

"I'll miss you, Estelle." Della told me. Her face had regained color, and she was breathing at a normal pace again.

I smiled at them. "I'm sorry I have to say goodbye so quickly."

"We understand." Raymond responded. The blood on his face had dried from the long drive, and his mother came up to him carrying a wet washcloth.

"I'll write to both of you." I promised. I reached out my hand to both of them. They both grabbed it, and squeezed it. I felt a tear run down my cheek.

"Thank you for everything." I told them. They both nodded at me.

Father started the car again, and Mother sat in the front seat, drifting off to sleep. I watched as Raymond's house left my sight. We drove through the streets of Boston for the last time, and I watched Mother in the front seat the entire drive. She was holding onto the little clay bird.

Acknowledgments

Thank you to my dad, for inspiring me to write this book and for paying for this whole project. Thanks to Cynde Christie, for editing this whole book and strengthening my writing skills. And thank you to Nick Zelinger, for the amazing cover art and title.

Thank you to Somie for dealing with my stress bombs. Thanks to Sienna Verma and Valentina McAree, for day-dreaming about my story in the middle of the night with me, and making me truly excited about it. Thank you to Mrs. Macalik and Mr. Dalrymple, for being my English teachers. Thank you to Mrs. Rezakhani for helping me schedule my time during my study halls. Thank you to Zara Miah for helping me choose between all of the amazing cover design choices. Finally, thanks to Tiffany Cung for helping me pick out character names all the way back in April.

About the Author

Myra Lee Glass is a young adult author who lives in Texas with her parents and sister. *A Daughter's Journey* is her first novel.

To connect with Myra,
visit www.MyraLeeGlass.com

Although this is a work of fiction, depression is a very real illness. If you or a loved one experience depression, please seek help from a professional in your area.